The Whistlers in the Dark

Victoria Williamson

Scotland Street Press

First Published in the UK in 2023 by
Scotland Street Press
100 Willowbrae Avenue
Edinburgh EH8 7HU

A CIP record of this book is available from the British Library

ISBN 978-1-910895-80-1

Cover, illustration and title lettering design by Elise Carmichael
Back cover arrangement by Mirrin Hutchinson
Typeset by Thomas Pearson

LOTTERY FUNDED

For my secondary school history teacher, Mr Roberts, who was as enthusiastic in his teaching as he was inspiring, and who made his engaging lessons something to look forward to each week.

Jinny

They said his death were all my fault.

But it weren't. It were all that Roman boy's fault. He's the one who started it. If it weren't for him, my wee brother would still be running alongside me up the braes like he used to, and I would've been affirmed a woman of the village with the rest of my age-mates long afore now. Instead of that I'm stuck a wee lassie till I can prove I'm no just a trouble-maker with a firebrand temper and a gift for making mischief. It's no going to be easy, no now I've got a hankering worse than hunger to make that Roman boy pay for what he went and did to my wee brother Bram. I've been biding my time, but now the autumn leaves are blowing and the winds are whistling over the fields, and the season's ripe for me to get my revenge.

My name's Jinny. I'm twelve autumns old, and this is the story of how I woke the sleeping stones and brought fire and destruction down on us all.

Chapter One

Jinny

'Jinny, be a good lass and nip up the Tintock Brae to see if there's any brambles left afore the metal men strip the bushes,' Ailsa said, shoving an empty basket at me like there weren't no way I'd be daft enough to refuse her.

I dropped the turnip I'd been peeling into a bucket and scowled at her. Picking berries weren't no job for a grown woman, and we both knew it. Besides, down in the valley by Tintock Brae, the ancient circle of stones stood shivering in the mist, and I weren't fool enough to want to go stomping up the hill and risk waking them this close to the Samhain festival. In just a few short sundowns, the veil between our world and the spirit realm would part and all manner of dark creatures would go flitting about the night. Maybe even the sleeping stones would rouse themselves and go walking. I shuddered at the thought. It weren't that I were afeared of them exactly, I weren't no wee lassie listening all wide-eyed to the stories on my ma's knee no more. But I weren't going to go volunteering for no bramble-picking run up the brae afore Samhain neither.

'I'm busy,' I said, tapping the big pile of turnips Ma had pulled up from the field. 'Can't you send one of the bairns? They've no got anything better to do.'

A group of boys were having a wooden sword fight by the grain store, the wee lassies egging them on and chucking turf clods to keep the battle going. It were just a game, but it made me sad to see. I weren't a bairn like them no more, but I weren't a woman neither. The shame of missing the coming-of-age ceremony on account of my part in my brother's accident were bad enough, but that weren't all that troubled me. The sadness ran deep as the dyke that the Romans had built right across our land, cutting us off from the best grazing pastures for our sheep and herding us like cattle into our villages north of the wall. The great wall were put up afore I were even born, but the bitterness it caused filled me like poison, sickening me every time I thought on how they treated my tribe and disrespected our land.

'Come on then, you ugly metal man!' a big lump of a lad yelled at one of the smaller bairns. 'Let's see how you like the taste of my sword!' He poked the wee boy a bit too hard with his stick and the bairn started howling.

'It's no fair! How come I always have to be a metal man? I'm no a nasty Roman! Ailsa, tell him it's no fair.'

'Right, that's enough all of you!' Ailsa heaved herself off her stool and glared at the bairns with her one good eye. She'd got a club foot and had gone half blind, but that didn't stop Ailsa from being the fiercest old woman in the whole village. She could even put the fear of death in the full-grown warriors when she were in the mood for it.

'Put them sticks and clods down and stop making mischief. Nyle, a big lad like you ought to be looking after the sheep, no beating wee bairns to a pulp. Take them wee boys with you and get yourself out on the sheiling with the shepherds. Birgit, Mavie, you two come over here and help me strip these willow rods for baskets.'

The bairns all groaned and dragged their feet, but they did what they were told all the same. Ailsa weren't the head of our village, but when it came to giving orders, that didn't make two sticks of difference. I sat smirking at the wee lassies stripping the willows right up until Ailsa added under her breath, 'Jinny, them brambles are no going to pick themselves.'

I pretended I didn't hear. Peeling turnips weren't much fun, but at least it weren't a bairn's job that'd leave me red-faced in front of my age-mates. I glanced over at the group of four new-made women who were sitting on stools at the weaving shed. Coira and Ethne were both thirteen springs old, one as tall as a rowan tree, the other short and round like a cider barrel. They leaned over the loom taking turns to run their shuttles through the warp and weft, the tartan cloth growing like magic beneath their fingers. Ennis, the loom master, beamed at them like they were the best pupils he'd ever taught. I glowered at his back, my breath curdling in my throat with resentment. He'd never looked at me like that. And my cheek still stung from the slap I'd got the other day when I sneaked a go at the loom and got the threads all tangled.

Rhona, twelve autumns old and pretty as a patch of heather, were carding thick clumps of wool between two wooden paddles, biting her lip with effort as she teased the fibres apart. Mairi sat beside her, her spindle twirling to the ground as she wound the long threads up the wooden shaft. It were Mairi that made me madder than all the rest put together. It weren't her fault, no really. But she were only eleven winters old, see, and she were made a woman along with the rest of them at the Bairntime's Passing ceremony five new moons ago. And here I were, a full season older than her, no invited to a confirmation ceremony to make me a woman yet, and still a wee lassie in the eyes of the Council. I could still remember the way the Elders' eyes scowled at me in the firelight the night of the accident. My heart were already half broken over Bram, and I'd never forget the pain of it snapping clean in two when they told me I weren't fit to be a woman of the village...

'They killed him!' I yelled at the Council leaders, 'in their pits filled with big wooden stakes! That Roman boy chased us right in!'

The two Roman soldiers might as well have been made out of fire-cast iron for all the difference my words made to them. They muttered a bunch of things under their breath, all lofty and impatient like they'd got better things to do than explain themselves to us ignorant villagers. We waited an age, impatient to hear about their part in the death and how they came to be carrying my wee brother's broken body home from the pits they'd dug in front of their great wall. Then that nasty wee Roman boy translated it into our language for us, and my hands curled into fists of rage at his lying words.

'The Damnonii tribe boy and his sister were hunting on our land,' he said, too much of a coward to meet my eyes. 'They stole two rabbits from our hunting dogs and ran off with them. We only wanted to recover what was ours from the thieves, nothing more.'

'LIARS!' I shrieked, the fury of the four winds in the very teeth of winter full upon me. 'This is no your land, it's OURS! Just 'cause you came marching up here with your swords and shields and your stupid Roman laws and built that accursed wall right across our homeland, that don't make it yours any more than it makes our rabbits and deer yours! You're nothing but lying, stinking THIEVES!'

I lunged at the Roman boy, seeing as he were my height and I had better odds of getting my hands around his neck and squeezing the life out of him than the metal men. My pa got to me afore I made it halfway round the campfire, though, dragging me back so I couldn't make more mischief. He kept his big arms clamped tight round my shoulders while the Council Elders muttered with their heads pressed close together and their eyes dark as the night sky. I could feel all the muscles in Pa's arms twitching, like he were fit to burst under the strain of holding me close to him. It were only when I glanced up and saw the stricken look on his face that the full force of my misdeeds hit me. I'd never seen Pa so hurt and scared looking afore. He weren't just grieving for Bram; he were grieving for me and my punishment that were still to come.

Oh, spirits of the autumn that gave me life, save me now, I thought. I were in so much trouble, I were half afraid to breathe in case each new gulp of air I took were destined to be my last. The Council leaders were siding with the Romans, and my fate were sealed. I were going to be publicly punished – flung as an offering on the bonfire of their cowardice so they could keep the fragile peace with our invaders.

Our village chief got up from his stool at long last, his face like storm clouds thick with rain. 'Donall,' he said to Pa, 'we're truly sorry about Bram. But your Jinny has brought us close to another war with her thoughtlessness. She's got too much of the flighty autumn bird in her and she needs to be punished. We can do no less or these metal men will go back to their fort and bring the whole army down on our heads.'

Gregor didn't like saying the words any more than Pa liked hearing them, but he kept going all the same. The Roman soldiers were watching with their heads bent to catch the translation from the boy who'd caused all the trouble in the first place. They started nodding in satisfaction when they heard what Gregor and the Council had decided.

'Jinny, you're no fit to be a woman of this village, no yet and probably no for a long time to come,' Gregor said heavily. 'You'll miss this year's Bairntime's Passing ceremony and stay a wee lassie in the eyes of the Damnonii tribe till such a day as you can prove you're no just a thoughtless bairn. You've brought trouble down on us all, and no end of grief to your parents this day.'

It were like he'd just announced my death to the whole tribe. But it weren't his words I took heed of just then, even though they cut me to the quick. It weren't even the sneers of the Roman soldiers nor the smug look of that wicked boy who'd caused all my suffering. No. It were the realisation that I'd had something more precious to me than all the gold in all the world taken from me that day, and I weren't ever going to get him back.

My losses hit me all at once like an arrow through my heart. My legs buckled under me and I slumped in Pa's arms, retching into the grass while he stroked my hair and tried to lift me back up with shaking arms. I couldn't hear his voice, though. All I could hear were Ma's screams in our hut as she leaned over the broken body of my wee brother.

'Bram!' she howled so fierce with despair it seemed the

very wind stopped still to listen. 'My baby, Bram! How could they do this to my bonnie wee bairn?'

The Roman soldiers didn't stay to hear her sobs. They just sheathed their swords and marched back to the safety of their fort beyond their great wall, leaving us to deal with the destruction they'd caused.

I vowed then and there I'd never forgive them as long as I lived.

And I would pay that Roman boy back double what he'd done to me and Bram...

'Well, Jinny? Are you just going to sit there dreaming all day or are you going to get up Tintock Brae like I told you and get them brambles picked?' Ailsa had her 'this is your final warning, girl' look on her face and I knew I'd pushed my luck too far already.

'Alright, alright I'm going,' I grumbled, shouldering the basket and stomping off afore I could catch sight of the pitying looks my age-mates were throwing me.

It weren't pity that were going to set all my wrongs to rights afore the autumn were over.

It were revenge.

Felix

She said his death was all my fault.

But it wasn't. She's the one who started it. If it wasn't for her tribe being so stubborn about a stretch of land that wasn't worth spitting on never mind dying for, my father would never have been posted to this godless wasteground, and I'd have been born to a Roman woman in the most amazing city on earth. Instead, my father's legion was ordered north to suppress the unconquered tribes beyond the river. There, I was born to a Damnonii woman who taught me the language and the local customs before she died of a fever. I wish she hadn't. Taught me, I mean. I wish with all my heart my mother hadn't died either, but it was teaching me the language that caused all the trouble in the first place. If I hadn't made friends with that Damnonii boy, Bram, then none of this would ever have happened. He was the one who showed me where the best hunting grounds were. I shouldn't have taken those soldiers there that day, I know that now. But Jinny shouldn't have tried to stop us taking those rabbits either. They belonged to Rome now, just like her tribe's land.

My name is Marcus Lucius Aquila Felix. I'm thirteen years old, and this is the story of how I had to choose between my Roman and my Damnonii roots in the war for the northern heartlands, when stone giants woke and came walking through the night.

Chapter Two

Felix

'Felix, the Quartermaster's out of relish again – go and see if you can find some of those wild berries north of the wall.' Capito swung the basket at me so hard it hit me full in the stomach. I bent over with a grunt, half-winded but trying not to show him it hurt.

'You're not the boss of me, Capito. If the Quartermaster wants berries, he can send one of the slaves for them.' I sounded braver than I felt. Kaeso Cassius Brutus wasn't someone who liked hearing the word 'no'. He thought he was boss of the whole world. That was why his nickname was Capito – 'large headed one' – seeing as he had such a big head.

Capito glowered at me and swung the basket again, but this time I managed to dodge out of the way. 'Leave me alone, Capito, I'm trying to study,' I said, showing him the history tablet I was holding. It was only a half-truth. What I'd really been doing for most of the morning was standing on the turf ridge of the wall, staring out over the wooden palisade and wondering if I was ever going to see my father again. He'd been sent out on a scouting party to the far north eight months ago, and no one had heard from him since.

'My father's the Senior Centurion of the second Augustan legion, and I'm ordering you to go and get those berries!' Capito took another step towards me, brandishing the basket like a weapon.

'My father's the Camp Prefect, he outranks your father,

and I'm telling you to get stuffed!' I snapped back.

'Your father,' Capito sneered, 'isn't here.'

I couldn't take it anymore. That smug face surrounded by its halo of blond curls was just begging to be punched. It didn't matter that Capito was a whole head taller than me, I took a swing at him anyway, a thrill of satisfaction running through me when my fist glanced off his jaw. My victory only lasted for the brief moment it took for Capito to recover and slam me to the ground. He sat on my chest and rained punches down on my head, and suddenly taking him on in a straight fight didn't seem like such a good idea after all.

'What's going on here?'

The thump of leather boots rounded the corner of the barrack block, and a moment later Appius Cassius Brutus was staring down at us, a file of legionaries fresh out of morning training lined up behind him. Capito's father had a neck as thick as a bull's, his brow so heavy over his beady eyes he had to get a helmet specially made to fit by the armour smith. The full force of that suspicious stare was turned on me now, and I gulped, pushing Capito off me and struggling back to my feet. Capito found an excuse before I could get the truth out. He always did.

'The Quartermaster needs relish for the meal tonight, and when I told Felix to gather berries, he attacked me!' he whined. 'This half-tribe boy's not fit to live in our fort, Father! He's a savage like those barbarians north of the wall, he ought to be out there living in their huts instead of here wasting our food.'

'I'm not a slave!' I spluttered angrily. 'My father's the Camp Prefect of this fort, and I'm not taking orders from the son of a centurion.' I should've bit my tongue and stopped it from coming out, but there was no swallowing the stupid words back down now.

Both Brutus and Capito bristled like wolves tensing for the hunt. 'I'm the Senior Centurion of the second Augustan legion, boy, you will show me some respect,' Brutus growled, crowding me back against the wall of the barracks until the metal buckles of his breastplate bit into my arms and I could smell the cider on his foul breath. 'I'm acting Camp Prefect until they declare your father dead, and you'd better get used to taking orders or you'll find yourself flushed out of here along with the rest of the camp sewage.'

'My father's not dead, he's coming home soon!' I protested. 'And I'm every bit as much a Roman as Capito is!'

Brutus sneered at that. 'Your mother was no citizen of Rome, just some savage Damnonii woman. Your father was a good man, a good soldier, but now he's a dead man and a dead soldier. Best accept it, boy, and learn your place.'

Capito sniggered as his father snatched my tablet and thrust the basket at me. I took it meekly, my cheeks burning in shame. Capito's mother was from this wild island of Britannia too, but she was from the southern conquered lands, and she spoke Latin well enough to be the chief gossip-merchant this side of the wall. That made Capito more of a Roman than I'd ever be. With my father gone and my Damnonii mother dead these last two years, I was in serious danger of being kicked out of the fort to fend for myself if I didn't prove I had what it took to be a Roman soldier when I finished school. And that meant following orders.

I choked back all my humiliation and resentment and

slung the basket over my shoulder, hurrying off before Brutus changed his mind and found an even worse job for me, like cleaning the latrines or slopping out the pig farm. I kept my head down all the way past the Commander's house and the legion headquarters, hoping I wasn't going to bump into any of the Tribunes or worse, their brat children. The noblemen kept themselves apart from the rest of us commoners in their fancy apartments filled with slaves and as many home comforts as the supply wagons could transport. It was bad enough Brutus was after my father's job and Capito wouldn't give me peace for five minutes together – now I had to watch my step around the Tribunes after that trouble over the Damnonii hunting grounds seven months back. There hadn't been a war with the local tribe in over fifteen years, not since the foundation stones were laid for the Antonine Wall. But I'd very nearly helped start a new one, and all for the sake of a couple of skinny rabbits hardly worth the trouble of cooking.

I waved my basket at the guards at the gate, and they nodded at me, lifting the heavy crossbar that held the huge doors shut and letting me through. It was mostly only legionaries on patrol who went north of the wall, but since they used me as a translator any time they had business with the local tribe, I was the only boy allowed out past the wall without special permission. Sometimes, like now, it was to pick berries or gather crab apples and nuts. But other times it was just to escape the confines of the camp and feel the wild north wind on my face.

I tramped across the bridge, hearing the wood creak beneath my leather boots. Beyond the wide ditch were the long patches of uneven ground where turf clods hid the sticks and leaves covering the deep defence pits. *Lilia* pits they were called, but the innocent-sounding name and heaps of autumn leaves hid the terrible danger lurking below. The pits were full of thick, sharpened stakes strong enough to pierce the skull of any warrior who dared sneak up on the wall in a surprise ambush.

Or slice clean through the limbs of a boy who stumbled on them unawares.

It wasn't my fault, I told myself for the thousandth time since the accident. *I never meant for him to get hurt.* But the skeleton trees of the copse where it all began rose into view, and at the top of a small mound the wind picked up, whistling round my head and rustling the autumn leaves strewn on the ground below.

I was there, it whispered in my ears. *I saw it all. I heard you share Bram's secret.*

'It wasn't my fault!' I said aloud. 'It was Jinny's fault!'

But the wind and I both knew I wasn't as innocent as I wanted to believe...

If my father hadn't already been gone a whole month before the accident, it never would have happened. I was lonely, and making friends with that Damnonii boy seemed like the best thing that had happened to me in ages.

'Race you to the hallowed tree!' Bram yelled over his shoulder. 'Last one there has to pay a forfeit!'

He took off like a fox on a mouse hunt, all tousled red hair and grinning white teeth. He was only ten years old, but by Mercury, that boy was fast.

'Hey! That's not fair, you had a head start! Bram, wait!'

I threw down the stick we'd been using to poke holes in

the frozen pond looking for fish and raced after him. There wasn't a hope I was going to catch him. But that's what I liked about Bram. He was like a bright patch of sunlight streaming through the grey clouds, always somewhere up ahead but never quite close enough to reach. You heard his laugh from a distance before you ever caught sight of him, and he stayed just long enough to bury you knee-deep in some fantastical story of goblins and fairies before he was off again, running on to the next adventure. Even in the depths of winter he was like the promise of spring just over the horizon. Not like his sister. She was all suspicious grey eyes and pursed lips beneath her mop of dark red hair. She was an autumn child alright, and she was sharp and frosty with the threat of coming winter always on her tongue. I stayed as far away from her as I could.

'You're too slow, Roman boy!' Bram laughed, reaching the huge oak that spread its branches far out over the meadow and slapping its thick trunk.

'You cheated!' I grumbled, slumping against the tree and panting as I finally caught up.

'You're a sore loser, Roman boy.'

'Don't call me that. My name's Felix.'

'What's that supposed to mean anyhow?'

'It's Latin for "luck".'

'You're no so lucky when it comes to running races,' Bram laughed, ''cause now you owe me.'

'What is it you want this time?' I groaned. But I wasn't sorry I came last, not really. Sometimes I lost bets to him on purpose just so I could see his face light up in delight when I smuggled little treats out of the camp for him in forfeit.

'Can you get me some of them sweet chestnuts you brought last time?'

'No can do, little man,' I shook my head.

'Aw, please? We've no got any nice things in our village now, what with winter clinging on so long and spring being shy about showing her face. The last of the crab apples were gone an age ago, and my tongue's hankering for the taste of something better than dried fish.'

'I know, it's the same at the fort,' I sighed, drawing my cloak further round my shoulders and stamping my feet to keep out the chill. My woollen tunic was made by the best cloth merchant the army could find between the wall in the south and the new wall in the north, but it wasn't a match for the thick tartan cloak and heavy trousers the Damnonii boy wore. 'We've been dining on cow's shin stew and pickled cabbage for the last two months now.'

'Liar!' Bram snorted. 'I can see all the way down into your precious fort from the top of Tintock Brae, and there's more cows and pigs in that field out back than my whole tribe could eat in a month of summers.'

'The livestock are mostly for the Tribunes and their families,' I shrugged. 'They get the best of everything. The centurions and soldiers come next since they need to stay strong for fighting, and the rest of us have to make do with what's left.'

'What's "Tribunes"?' Bram asked, rolling his tongue round the unfamiliar Latin word.

'You know, the noblemen? They're the ones in charge of the legion.'

'I thought you said centurions were in charge of the soldiers?'

'Yes, but someone has to be in charge of the centurions, don't they? There's six Tribunes, and the Legate's the commander of the whole legion.'

'Sounds bothersome.' Bram scratched his head, his eyes already roaming the frosty scrubland in search of a new adventure. 'So, your pa's not a Tribune, is he? Else you'd be getting good food too. Is he a centurion, then?'

'He used to be. He was Senior Centurion of the second Augustan legion till he was promoted a couple of years ago. Now he's the Camp Prefect of the fort. It's just one step below a Tribune, and he's in charge of the soldiers' training.' I couldn't keep the pride from my voice, and Bram's eyes slid sideways, grinning at me when he saw how puffed out my chest had become.

'Braggart!' he laughed. 'If he's such a big-chief-camp-commander man then how come you're no eating deer heart and pig's liver every night?'

'It's complicated,' I shrugged. 'My father's been sent north on a scouting trip to map out the wild mountain lands, and nobody likes me as my mother was a Damnonii woman, and the Senior Centurion hates me because he wants my father's position, and his son won't stop beating me up whenever we meet, and...' It all came out in a rush like cider spilling out of a leaky barrel before drying to a trickle. Somehow I couldn't keep my mouth shut around the friendly Damnonii boy – he always seemed to see right inside my head whether I spoke out loud or not.

Bram nodded and thumped my shoulder in sympathy. I wasn't sure he understood, not really, but his smile made me feel warm inside despite the chill winter wind.

'You want to know a secret?' he grinned after a long

pause.

'What kind of secret?'

'The kind of secret that'll fill your belly up with rabbit stew till the spring brings the foxes and badgers out of their holes again.'

'I'm listening.' I stopped stamping my cold feet and gazed eagerly at him instead.

'Ah, but you can't tell. Never ever, promise? 'Else them metal men will be all over it like an itchy rash and I'll never get to catch rabbits in there again.' Bram's eyes were bright in the pale sunlight. His kind heart was eager to share his secret with me, but his head was warning him not to give up something so precious in case I ruined it.

He should have listened to his head.

'I won't tell anyone. Not ever,' I said solemnly.

'Then follow me! Catch me if you can...'

Bram took off across the grass again, and this time I kept pace right alongside him all the way to the copse...

The copse was still there. The army had stripped most of the trees from the land north of the wall for the palisade that stretched across the top, but they left some of the younger saplings that weren't tall enough yet to be used for fencing. And they left the Damnonii's hallowed meeting tree in place, of course. There'd be war for sure if the Romans took so much as a splinter from its ancient trunk.

I stood at the top of the small rise, looking down at the spindly trees that hid the burrows crammed full of rabbits sheltering from the wind. I wished now the soldiers had torn down the trees of the copse a long time ago and found the burrows all by themselves. Then I wouldn't feel so guilty for telling them Bram's secret.

I knew I promised him that I wouldn't. But my father was gone, and I was scared and lonely and I just wanted them all to like me, to fit in. To be a *Roman*. I thought if I told Brutus, he'd stop bullying me and Capito would leave me alone. I was wrong. I made everything so much worse. I didn't cause the accident, not directly, Jinny was wrong to blame me for that. But if I hadn't shared Bram's secret hunting place with Brutus then none of us would've found ourselves in the wrong place at the wrong time.

And I was sorry for that, Bram. Believe me, I was so, so sorry.

Chapter Three

Jinny

I missed him so much sometimes it hurt to breathe.

Times like now, when I were clambering up Tintock Brae, the wind in my hair and the brambles catching at my skirts, and I were remembering the last time I went berry picking with Bram and Raggy. Bram were up to his usual tricks, tearing up the hillside like his backside were on fire then rolling down head over heels to land in a muddlesome heap, panting and helpless with laughter. How he didn't end up with his head broken into pieces, I'll never know. Raggy ran up and down between us till he were out of breath, then came and lay down beside me, licking the bramble juice off my hands with his rough tongue and nuzzling my legs till I gave in and stroked his ears.

He were the runt of the litter, Raggy were, his skinny wee body all pink like a plucked chicken when he finally came out a good half-night after the rest of the litter. Calan, the blacksmith, were going to dunk him in a water bucket to save him from suffering, but I were having none of it. I'd been promised a pup, and as soon as I set eyes on Raggy, I knew he were mine to keep. He were too weak to suck, so I made a thin soup out of milk and egg and dripped it into his wee mouth till he stopped shaking and went to sleep in my hand, his belly fat as a sheep's bladder. I sent the herders half barmy with begging for milk for a whole new moon, but it were worth their curses and slaps whenever I pinched a mug of clotted cream.

Every day I watched over Raggy like a mother hen sitting on a clutch of eggs, and got my reward when he finally opened his big brown eyes and looked at me for the very first time like I were the most wondrous thing in all the world. He needed help with feeding for a good bit longer, and I ducked every chore I could to check on him in the basket by my bedroll in the back of the hut. Ma weren't happy keeping him indoors, but that spring the winds were wild enough to shake big clumps of thatch off the roof, and I weren't going to tie him to a post outside and let him shiver himself to death in that bluster. Folks all laughed like I were soft in the head for doting on such a wee runt not worth the scrap of blanket he were wrapped in, but I knew better. I paid them no heed, smiling secretly to myself as I skimped each meal to feed Raggy scraps from my bowl.

By the time four springs had rolled right around, folks had long stopped laughing. My dog were the biggest of the hunting pack, with jaws that could crunch the leg of a stag clean in two with one bite. He were a big softie, though, and wouldn't hurt so much as a hair on a bairn's head. But he loved the chase, did Raggy, and he could outsprint a hare on flat ground going full pelt. That were why I took him with us that day, seven new moons ago now, when we went to the copse hunting rabbits. If I'd only left him at home with the rest of the pack, what happened to Bram would never have come to pass.

Jinny, there's no use thinking on it, you'll no change what's happened with all the wishing in the world, I told myself, setting my basket down and stretching my cramped legs as I reached the crest of the high hill. For all my crabbing to Ailsa about berry picking being bairns' work, I weren't sorry to have come. The top of Tintock Brae were just about my most favourite place in all the world, and standing high above the grasslands with the wind nipping my ears and the tang of berries sharp on my tongue were one of the keenest pleasures I could ever think of knowing.

To the north beyond the rough wooden posts that marked the boundary of our village were the sheilings where my tribe set the sheep to pasture and herded their cattle. Past them, the land rose up in the great humpbacked mounds of the Camsith Fells. On a clear winter day, the hills were cloaked in mantles of snow that shimmered like starlight in the pale rays of dawn. When the spring thaws came, the meltwater roared down the slopes, swelling the burns that crossed the pastureland and flooding the banks of the Luggie where I washed our clothes. Most folks loved the summertime the best, when the hills were green and fresh with life. But me, I were an autumn lass, born when the berries were full to bursting and the barley harvest lay four legs deep in the grain store.

It were mid-autumn now and the hills were still green, but the sky were flecked with grey clouds that rolled down from the north. I drew in a deep breath of the fresh breeze, knowing if I lingered over the gathering long enough, I'd be rewarded with the sight of the hills and pasturelands turning to beaten gold as the sun went down in the west. It made my heart ache with the beauty of it, and I'd risk a hundred of Ailsa's sharpest tongue-lashings just to dawdle up here till the shadows of dusk chased the last of that fairy light away.

But right now, bairns' work or no, I had a job to do. With a last look at the hills, I set my dreaming by and got to work, searching the tangled bushes for late berries over-looked in the earlier harvests. There weren't so many this year. The summer had been short and damp, the sun too shy to stay for long enough to keep the berries from spoiling. The north side of the brae had been picked clean, and the brambles left on the crest were soft and fell apart between my fingers. I gathered what I could, though, knowing every bit of food helped put off the day we had to start into our winter rations. Too early, and we'd be thin as reeds and weak with hunger by the time spring brought fresh grass to tempt the game out of their underground hideouts. We couldn't risk killing off too much of our sheep and cattle now the Romans had gone and cut us off from our hunting grounds in the south, and if we roamed further north than the Campsith Fells, the fierce warriors of the Maeatae tribe would soon send us running home again.

'Ow! The four winds blast you dratted wee bleeders to dust!' I cursed. 'Look what you've gone and done to my hand!'

I'd pricked my finger reaching for the berries hidden deep in the bush, and in my hurry to jerk my arm back, I'd scraped a big gash down the length of my palm. As I stood sucking the red drops that sprung up, a loud honking overhead made me turn my face to the sky. A flock of wild geese were heading south, riding the wind with their necks outstretched and their wings beating hard against the air. I followed them with my eyes, wondering where they were headed and what they'd see when they got there. Past Tintock Brae they flew, beyond the great turf wall that cut our land clean in two. The 'Antonine Wall' them metal men called it. But we had names of our own:

Dead Men's Mound.

Grim's Dyke.

The Wall of Tears.

That Roman wall were an ugly scar that they said sealed the fragile peace between us and them. They were too blind to see the maggots of resentment that squirmed and wriggled just beneath the skin of that peace, waiting for the chance to break free. One day soon, a war would come: whether the metal men started it, or whether the Damnonii did, the end would be the same. That turf wall were going to come tumbling down, along with the great forts where their army skulked like rats in a grain store, getting fat off our land and labour.

From the heights of Tintock Brae, I could just see over the line of fencing that topped the turf wall, to the wooden stockade that hid the army of metal men from even the keenest Damnonii eyes. I couldn't make out no more than that. Them Romans weren't daft. They built their wall and their fort on the highest ground they could find, save for the hilltop where I stood now. 'Caerpen Taloch' we called the great wooden city south of our village – 'the fort at the end of the hill'. It marked the edge of my world. I'd never get the chance to journey further south in my lifetime now that them metal men had blocked off the path to the distant horizon. It made me mad to think of them fencing me in like some tame wee lamb on my own land.

The wild geese were mad too. They honked and hissed as they soared above the great wall, their wings beating the air with frantic strokes. But then a group of archers scrambled up the back of the turf wall on the Roman side, and I knew then that the geese weren't mad; they were scared. The metal men raised their bows, and a hail of arrows streaked through the sky, scattering the birds in a shrieking muddle. Two were brought down straight off, a third limping through the air with a broken wing till it gave up the struggle halfway over the fort. From high on Tintock Brae, I could almost hear the metal men cheering. Almost.

Them birds don't belong to the metal men any more than our land does! I thought, fury boiling my blood as I watched the last bird stagger from the sky. *They're murdering thieves, and they're no going to stop till every last one of us is dead and gone along with our game.*

Our game. They took them birds as if they owned the skies, just like they took the rabbits that day as if they owned the secret copse...

'Hurry, Jinny! Raggy's got the scent and he's closing in!' Bram yelled, looking back over his shoulder as he ran, his blue eyes bright in the spring sunshine. I almost laughed at how red his face had gone with excitement. He loved the thrill of the chase every bit as much as Raggy did.

'I'm coming!' I panted. 'Wait for me!'

I could run up and down the braes till the cows came home, but I'd never hope to match the speed of Bram and Raggy. Them two could beat a hare by half a sheiling's length in a straight race. I could see the rabbit up ahead, bolting for the cover of the copse. Raggy were close on its tail, his neck straining and his legs flashing past in a blur of brown fur. He reached the copse at the same time the rabbit did, and he and Bram disappeared behind the screen of young trees. There were silence for a brief moment, like everything under the sun were holding its breath to see what the outcome would be.

And then the yelling started. Loud and angry. And mostly in Latin.

That were when I dropped the leather pouch of skinning tools I'd been holding and made a dash for the copse like my legs were on fire.

'Bram!' I yelled, my mind in a panic at what I might find. 'Bram? What's happening?'

I soon found out.

There were two metal men in the copse with the brown-skinned Roman boy I'd warned Bram a thousand times to stay away from. One of the soldiers had Bram by the scruff of the neck, shaking him so hard his teeth were clattering like hail off a metal bucket. The other soldier were holding a couple of chains attached to the nastiest pair of hunting dogs I'd ever set eyes on. It were lucky I'd got the blacksmith to make Raggy a spiked collar to tie round his neck just in case he ran afoul of wolves when we were out hunting. One of the dogs had plainly tried to take a bite out of Raggy's neck, for his muzzle were red raw with gashes and blood drooled from his mouth. I grinned at that. That Roman dog didn't like the taste of the collar any better than the wolves did.

'Get your manky great hands off him!' I yelled, lunging at the beetle-browed soldier who were jerking Bram about like a bairn's toy. But instead of dropping Bram, he grabbed me too, his fist catching hold of my hair and near pulling a clump out by the roots. 'Ow! Let go of me, you metal monster!'

The Roman boy started jabbering away in Latin just

then, and he must've been saying something awful funny about us, as the metal man holding me and Bram let out a big snort of laughter and shook us harder. Two rabbits lay dead at the soldier's feet, and I knew from the way Raggy were tensing and sniffing the air that one of them were the game he'd been chasing.

'Call your dog off,' the Roman boy said suddenly in our language. 'If he goes for the rabbit, it'll make everything worse.'

I didn't know what made me madder – him speaking our tongue like he were born to it, or him giving me orders. 'Go poke your eyes out, you wee Roman gob of spit! This is our land and our rabbits. Tell your metal men to hand them over or it'll be war for sure.'

The Roman boy's brown eyes widened like he were going to wet his breeches. That scared him alright. 'Please, stop struggling!' he said. 'You'll end up hurt! Bram, listen to me! Call that dog of yours off or they'll set the hunting hounds on him.'

'I'm no listening to you ever again!' Bram yelled, aiming a kick in the Roman boy's direction. 'I told you never to say nothing about this copse and now you've gone and ruined everything!'

'You told him about the copse?' I gasped, clawing at the soldier's fingers to try to free my hair. 'Bram! He's no one of us! He's a Roman!'

'I know that now,' Bram growled. 'C'mon Jinny, let's take what's ours and run for it!'

'No!' the Roman boy yelled, but it were too late. Bram and me both took big bites out of the soldier's hands, and he yelled like a squalling bairn and dropped us clean to the ground. Quick as a flash, we took to our heels. Raggy were smarter than both of them metal men put together, and he grabbed one of the rabbits in his jaws and took off with it like a bolt of lightning. I grabbed the other on the way past for good measure.

It were ours, I grinned to myself as I ran. *They've got no right taking what's meant for our cooking pot.*

The three of us hurtled through the trees and shot across the wide strip of land that swept up to the great turf wall. It weren't the best direction to run in, and there weren't no cover out in the open, but we couldn't double back till we'd cleared the base of Tintock Brae, else them fierce Roman dogs with their strong legs would catch us on the steep slopes. I weren't scared for my wee brother out in plain sight, though, no matter how close we got to the big wall that scowled down on us. There weren't no one faster than Bram and Raggy over level ground, and I weren't going to let nothing – dog nor Roman – get a hold of him again. I weren't half as quick, and I lagged behind by a good way, but I had a sharp knife in my pocket and a belly full of fire for a fight if need be.

As we skirted the wall, I heard a yell coming from some- where behind. Up ahead, Bram didn't hear, but I risked a glance back, wanting to know what we'd be up against. I thought the soldiers would be on us for sure, but they weren't chasing us, and better, they hadn't let loose their hunting dogs to run us down neither. They just stood at the edge of the copse watching us and pulling on their barking dogs' chains. It were that Roman boy who were doing the running after us for them, waving his arms like a chicken flapping on the chopping block. He were yelling something over and over, but I were too mad to hear him.

And that were when it happened.

That were when the ground opened up and swallowed my wee brother whole.

'Bram!'...

Bram! My wee Bram...

I passed a hand across my brow, feeling the sweat gathering there despite the chill in the air. The sun were high overhead, peeking out from behind thin wisps of cloud, not strong enough to warm my bones never mind bring my blood to the boil. Yet I were hot and restless none the less, the memories of that day bringing on a fever that made my skull pound and set my teeth on edge.

It were that Roman boy's fault, I thought darkly. *He were the one who chased us into the pits. Them soldiers were willing to let us go our way, but that wicked boy made sure we headed straight for the traps by the wall. I'll never forget what he did, and never forgive him.*

I snatched my basket up again and headed for the south slopes of the brae. I'd done my best with the slim pickings on the summit, and I could only hope the berries on the hillside nearest the wall had fared better in the damp. I'd only clambered over a big rock and taken three steps down the south slope when I came face to face with the last person in the whole world I wanted to see for as long as I lived.

'You!' I hissed, near dropping my basket in surprise.

The Roman boy blinked up at me with eyes as wide as wagon wheels.

Now! I said secretly, my hand reaching for the knife in my pocket. *Now the season's ripe for my revenge.*

Chapter Four

Felix

I stood there staring at her like I was frozen to the spot.

She was like Medusa from the old Greek myths, her hair a nest of red snakes that turned me to stone with one look.

'What are you doing here?' I gulped. As soon as it was out, I knew it was the wrong thing to say. Her grey eyes narrowed, her scowl so deep her forehead seemed to buckle under the weight of her anger.

'I got every right to go where I please,' she growled. 'This is our land, and them brambles belong to us!' She glared at the basket of berries I'd been picking. It was twice as full as her own. Her free hand began slowly reaching for the pocket of her skirt. She saw me looking and grinned, fierce and mean. I was pretty sure she kept her knife in there. I took a step back, forgetting for a moment I was standing on a steep slope. My foot found thin air instead of solid ground and I stumbled, my knee hitting the turf with a thump so sharp it might've broken if the grass hadn't been so damp.

Jinny's hand only briefly hesitated on its way to her pocket. Then, as fast as a viper, it changed tack and snatched at my basket instead. Before I could stop her, Jinny was off and running back up Tintock Brae, dodging in and out of the thorn bushes and disappearing over the hilltop. 'You want the brambles?' she called back gleefully. 'Then come and get them, Roman boy!'

'Those are mine!' I yelled, scrambling up and limping after her. 'Come back!'

She didn't listen.

She didn't listen last time either...

'Come back!'

The moment Bram and Jinny took off out of the copse, I knew they were heading in a dangerous direction. Brutus was about to set the hunting dogs loose on them, but when he saw which way they were running, he thought better of it.

'No point putting the beasts in harm's way,' he grinned, wiping the blood from his hands where two sets of teeth had broken the skin. 'We'll get those rabbits back as soon as those brats hit the *lilia* pits.'

The soldier with the other dog gave another nasty laugh, just like the one that had made Jinny so mad moments ago when I'd tried to ask Brutus to let her and Bram go. I was pretty sure she thought I'd been making a joke about her, but if she kept running towards the wall, it would be a lot more than her feelings that would get hurt.

'Come back!'

I raced out of the copse behind them, waving to get their attention. Bram was too far ahead with their dog to hear me, but Jinny turned to look back a couple of times without breaking stride. She heard me alright, but she just didn't listen.

'It's dangerous!' I shouted. 'You're running straight into the spike pits!'

I should've warned Bram about the *lilia* pits before now. It had been a long harsh winter and the soldiers were getting jumpy. Every fresh watch reported seeing shadows of warriors forming in the mist, getting ready to break the peace and attack. I knew it was probably the stale cider talking, but the centurions weren't about to take any chances. Under cover of darkness, a whole row of spike pits were dug in front of the wall at Caerpen Taloch fort and covered over so the warriors of the tribes wouldn't know they were there if they came to attack. The pits were meant to hold off grown men with swords and axes, not two children with a dog and a couple of stolen rabbits. But wooden stakes were dead things that didn't care whose bones they snapped in two. Brutus should've cared, though, he shouldn't have just stood there and watched from the copse like he'd got front row seats to a bear fight at the Colosseum.

'Come back!' I yelled again. 'You have to stop!'

I'd nearly caught up with Jinny when it happened.

One minute Bram and their dog were running across the open ground skirting the wall, the next there was a loud cracking of branches, a frightened yell, and Bram and the dog disappeared. My heart nearly stopped stone-still in fear. My feet slowed, and I had to force them to drag me forward to the edge of the pit, my breath coming in thick gasps with each step.

Jinny didn't know what was down there. Not yet. She raced to the spot where her brother had disappeared, throwing herself down on the grass and leaning over the edge of the yawning hole.

'Bram? Bram!'

Her next words were lost in a long, piercing shriek. She didn't stop screaming the whole time it took me to reach the pit and look down. I wished I hadn't. What I saw gave me nightmares. But for Bram's sake, I had to force myself to gaze into that deep, dark hole.

There was blood everywhere.

A tangle of limbs.

A scattering of broken stakes.

And down at the bottom of the pit, two dead eyes staring back up at us...

'Jinny! Come back!' I yelled, my knee throbbing painfully as I stumbled down the north side of the hill. 'I need those berries! I'll be in big trouble if I go back without them!'

She kept running, the colours of her thick tartan shawl fading into the grey mist that rose up from the river snaking through the valley. I slowed as I hit the wall of fog, damp fingers of vapour trailing across my cheek and down my spine, making me shiver in the sudden darkness. The sun disappeared as the mist rose overhead, the birdsong turning muffled and distorted until the only sound I could hear was my breath catching in my throat.

'Jinny? Where are you?'

My voice was swallowed by the mist as soon as the words left my mouth. I stopped, straining my ears for a response, but there was nothing but silence in the grey world around me. Silence and the dark shape that loomed ahead of me in the gloom.

'Jinny?'

But it wasn't her. The shape was too tall to be a girl. As soon as I saw it, I knew why she'd led me here. In my rush to recover the berries and avoid another run-in with Brutus, I'd clean forgotten why I never ventured down the north slope of this hill into the valley beyond. No one did. This was where the sacred stones of the Damnonii tribe stood. They were never to be disturbed, never to be woken by man or beast. And I'd gone and blundered right down into their midst.

That's when the fear took hold of me.

I backed away slowly, holding my breath so hard my lungs burned. If I was very, very careful then maybe I could get out of here before I woke the stones.

I'd barely taken five steps when I sensed something in the mist behind me. I froze, listening for the sound of breathing. But Jinny wasn't creeping up behind me either. It was something else. I tore my eyes from the stone in front of me for the brief moment it took me to glance behind. There in the gloom stood another dark shape, even taller than the first. Another stone was blocking my escape back up the hill. I whirled round, disoriented. I could've sworn it hadn't been there a moment before.

Maybe I didn't come that way after all, I thought, my mind in a panic. *Maybe I've just lost my sense of direction in the dark.* The thick mist rising from the river seemed to be seeping right through my skin, working its way inside my head and dulling all my senses. *Focus, Felix!* I told myself. *You have to get out of here!*

When I looked back at the first stone, it was closer than it had been before, I was sure of it. A cold blast of air lifted the dense fog for just a moment, and in the pale light I saw I was standing right in the centre of the sleeping stone circle. Then the darkness closed around me once more, trapping me there with no way to escape but to feel my way through the mist and risk running straight into one of the slumbering giants.

What if they wake up? I wondered, searching in my head for the story fragments my mother had told me. I knew the stones were sacred, I knew they were never to be disturbed. *But what happens if they are, Mother, what then?* I thought.

It was no use, the ending of the story just wasn't there.

The mist swirled again, and by the time it lifted, the stones had sleep-walked one step closer to me, I was certain of it now. They knew I was here, and their dreams were turning restless. I only had a few moments to escape before they woke to find me in their midst.

Run! I tried to order my shaking legs. *Get out of here!*

Before I could move, a soft whisper of laughter danced out of the gloom, mocking me, daring me to run. Then it began. Faintly at first, then rising to a shrill wail.

Whistling.

Jinny was whistling in the dark, waking the sleeping stones that surrounded me. I forgot all about my stolen basket of berries, not caring now if I returned without them, just as long as I escaped. I stumbled blindly through the mist, running for my life with the sound of whistling echoing in the darkness all around me.

Chapter Five

Jinny

It weren't his basket of brambles I wanted.

I just took that to get him to follow me.

No, what I wanted were the chance to get even. A life for a life, that were the only way to make things fair after what them Romans took from me in their spike pits. As soon as my hand went for the knife, I knew it were the wrong tool for the job. I weren't no evil metal man, and I'd no stomach for killing anything bigger than a rabbit. I couldn't hurt Felix, no with my own two hands. Besides, if them Romans found his body here all full of holes, they'd know it were one of us who had done it, and my whole tribe would suffer for it. No, there were a better way.

I snatched his basket and legged it down the north side of the brae, grinning when I heard him stumble after me all sore-kneed and out of breath. It seemed only right this were the way it were all to end, seeing as how Bram wouldn't never get to run by my side ever again.

The mist from the Luggie River hovered over the deep valley all year round even at the height of summer. Now it were autumn, the fog hung thick and heavy with menace, warning us off from the circle of sacred stones it protected. I weren't stupid, I knew it were a dangerous game I were playing as I ran full tilt into the gathering dark. But I also knew this were my best chance to get revenge for Bram and Raggy once and for all, and I weren't going to let no scary legends get between me and justice for them.

I slowed when I reached the stone circle, holding my breath tight as I crossed to the other side and slid down the bank of the Luggie. I set the baskets down and reached into my skirts, looking for the means to do what needed to be done. My hand brushed the handle of my knife again, but it were the weapon tucked below I were hunting for. I pulled my sling out slow and careful, feeling around in the wet grass for a rock that would fly straight and true till it smacked that Roman boy right between the eyes and knocked him out cold. With a bit of luck, when he woke up alone here in the dead of night, with the stones all around him in the dark, the fear of the place would stop his heart beating right there and then. His mother had been a Damnonii woman, so he knew the legends, same as us.

Same as us...

For a moment I hesitated, my hand fumbling in the grass. My ma said his mother were a good woman, but she'd been so in love with a metal man she'd given up her place in the tribe to go and live behind the wall with him. Maybe her son weren't all bad Roman. Maybe there were a bit of Damnonii in him too. After all, he could speak our language like he were born to it. And Bram had liked him better than any of his age-mates in our village. And...

Bram...

The anger flashed red hot through my veins again when I remembered what the Roman boy had done, and what it had led to. He deserved to be punished.

My hand found what it were looking for, the perfect gob of stone for the job. It were round and smooth, heavy enough to knock the nasty Roman boy senseless, but light enough to hurl from the leather pouch of my sling. I crouched low on the bankside and waited, my heart hammering with the thrill of the hunt.

Sure enough, a couple of quick heartbeats later, he came lumbering though the mist, calling for me to give his berries back like I were the thief instead of him. Huh, the arrogant wee maggot! It were bad enough he'd gone and told the metal men where our best rabbit-hunting grounds were to be found, now he were helping them strip Tintock Brae of our brambles and all. He'd be back at Caerpen Taloch fort tonight, feasting on them for sure. I saw an image in my head of him chewing juicy rabbit and deer while we went hungry, and snapping his fingers for slaves to come and fill his cup with cider made of apples stolen from our trees. It made me so mad I near made up my mind to toss my sling down and run him through with my knife and have done with it.

But no. This weren't just revenge for me. This were revenge for Bram. For his sake, I choked down my temper and bided my time, my fingers tight round the leather straps of my sling. It were hard to see in the dark, but the mist were on my side. Just when I needed to know where he were standing to aim my stone, it lifted for a brief moment and I caught a look at him. That were when I hesitated again. He had dark skin and black curly hair like his Roman father, but the way his eyes went wide when he saw he were slap-bang in the centre of the sleeping stone circle were pure Damnonii. No Roman would care about some big rocks and our tribe's legends. Maybe he were scared half senseless already, and that were punishment enough. Maybe I didn't need to knock him out so he'd wake cold and alone in the dark. Maybe thinking on him dying of fear as he stared up at the stones looming over him wouldn't make me feel good after all. Maybe...

One more look at them eyes of his made my mind up. For the first time it hit me: they were the exact same shade of brown as my Raggy's eyes. The anger surged through me again, hotter and faster this time as the memory of that day at the spike pits flashed afore me. The horrible pictures in my head of what I'd seen down there were all this Roman boy's fault. If I wanted rid of them nightmares, I needed rid of the cause. I needed rid of *him*. I crept back up the bank and tiptoed closer, careful to make no sound with my boots or wake the stones. I weren't so much of a fool for revenge as that.

I'd just drawn my sling back behind my head, when that great feather-brained Roman boy went and moved. And no just in any direction. He started backing up so close to one of the standing stones he near bumped right into it.

That were when the fear closed round my heart in a grip so tight, I couldn't hardly breathe with the pain of it. The cry of victory died in my throat, coming out choked like the laugh of a strangled cat.

Stop, you deadwit! I wanted to yell. *You'll wake them up!*

But I weren't so brain-addled with panic to do something as foolish as that. Instead, I did what I should've done as soon as I crossed the curtain of mist into the valley. I started to whistle. The sound were soft and shaky at first, gaining grit as the music drifted through the fog, lulling the stone giants back to sleep like I'd been taught since I were old enough to sit on my grandma's knee and hear her stories.

To be truthful, whistling's weren't exactly what I were

meant to do.

Grandma always said the stones were evil giants from the old days afore the metal men ever crossed over the seas. They were cursed by a Damnonii witch for their wicked child-killing ways, turned to stone and set to slumbering, waiting in the mist for unwary travellers to stumble into their circle so they could feast on their flesh. Ailsa said that weren't true at all, and the stones were sleeping Damnonii warriors, waiting for the day when our tribe reached its darkest hour of need. On that day, they'd rise up and walk the land once more to give us the help we needed. I weren't sure which tale to believe. Ailsa and my grandma argued over it every day till Grandma passed away, and even now Ailsa still had words with anyone who said the stones were pure evil.

But there were one thing that everyone agreed on. And that were the simple fact the stones needed to be kept asleep. No one were allowed in this patch of valley, no to fish, pick brambles, nor even to follow the path of game crossing through under cover of mist. I shouldn't be here. I were chancing my luck for sure. But if I smashed that Roman boy's head with a rock and he died of fright when he woke, then no one would ever be able to trace the deed back to me nor my tribe. It'd look for all the world like he stumbled into the mist unawares and hit his head on one of the great stones in the dark.

Just an accident. No one's fault.

Just like they said what happened to Bram were an accident.

If them liars could get away with their crime, then so could I. I just had to make sure I didn't do a worse thing than walking over sacred ground by waking the stone giants while I were here. And to keep them asleep, I had to whistle, like I'd been taught.

I hadn't been taught to whistle, no really. We'd all learned from our Elders that if we found ourselves in the valley by chance in the dark and were afeared of waking the stones, we'd to sing them back to sleep. Only, I had a voice like rusty nails scraping down the side of an old axe, so I were dead certain opening my mouth and screeching the tune out would wake them in a flash. So I whistled the song Grandma had taught me instead.

Hum me a tune, lad, whistle me home,
It's been a long time, lad, I'm worn to the bone.
My comrades have fallen, the peace pipes have cracked,
So hum me a tune, lad, whistle me back.

Sing me a song, lass, lull me to sleep,
I'm heartsick and weary, but too tired to weep.
The war drums are silent, the warriors dead,
So sing me a song, lass, lull me to bed.

The sound were eerie in the mist and muffled like I were covering my mouth with a thick blanket. I should've started whistling right when I first crossed the circle, but I didn't want to give the game away to the Roman boy afore he lost his way in the dark and stumbled after me. I could see him there in the drifting mist, gazing round like a mouse caught in the glare of a cat. He couldn't see me, but he were staring at the stones like he were sure they were closing in on him. They had that effect on folk.

The mist played tricks with your head till you thought you were gone half mad. But I held my nerve, whistling louder and swinging my sling round and round above my head, waiting for the moment to strike.

Just as I let fly with my rock, the stupid oaf went and moved. The sound of my whistling must've sent him over the edge of reason, for he let out a frightened yelp and bolted just as my rock went sailing through the air. My heart near jumped out of my mouth when I heard the sharp crack it made when it landed. It weren't the crack of stone on bone. It were the crack of stone on stone.

My legs were shaking so hard I couldn't hardly drag myself up the bank and through the mist to the spot where I were sure my rock had landed. The sight of the standing stone rearing out of the dark above me near made me empty my bladder there and then, but it were seeing the damage I'd done that sent me staggering back with my hand to my mouth.

I'd gone and knocked a great lump out of one of the sacred stones.

They'd stood there undisturbed for more winters than my tribe could count, and now a stupid wee spit of a lass who weren't even good enough to be a grown woman had gone and smashed a big chunk from one of the stones with her badly aimed revenge. I stopped whistling at the sight and cursed myself loudly in the dark.

And that were when I saw the stones move.

Two steps closer they came to me through the mist, I could've sworn my life on it. Faces scowled out of the crags in the rock, eyes that should've stayed closed for all time now open to glare at me. Maybe it were real, maybe it were all in my fevered head and I were seeing things in the dark that weren't there, just like I'd hoped the Roman boy would afore I punished him. But now the punishment were all mine, the fear were all mine, and the half sob of terror that followed me like a shadow as I fled through the mist were mine too.

I ran blind and stumbling from the circle, just like the boy had done moments afore, only in the other direction. Giving no heed to where I were headed, I tore through the mist, clawing past bramble bushes that got in my way and making for the last of the daylight that shone pale and sick at the edge of the fog line as the sun went down. My head were so full of fear and choked up with stories of ghouls that might drag me back into the dark, I near fainted afore I reached the safety of the valley pass.

Just as I crossed the damp grey curtain that marked the edge of the mist, another shape loomed up to stand between me and the setting sun, blocking the light from view. I yelled in fright, falling on my knees in front of the apparition.

It weren't a stone giant, nor the ghost of a metal man, nor the long dead remains of some poor soul drowned in the Luggie on a cold winter's day.

It were my wee brother, Bram.

Chapter Six

Felix

I knew she hated me after what happened to Bram. I just didn't know how much until now. *She's set the stone giants on me!* I panicked as I ran. *She's woken them up and now they're coming for me!*

I looked back every few steps, but all I could see was the tangle of berry bushes on the steep rise of Tintock Brae and the orange glow of the sun setting beyond the pasturelands on the western horizon. All was quiet, there was nothing behind me. But I knew they were coming for me all the same.

It was dark by the time I limped back to the wall, my knee aching and my hands trembling so hard it was an effort to pound my fist against the heavy wooden gate. I had to knock three times before the guard on duty grudgingly opened it for me.

'What are you doing skulking out there at this hour?' he grumbled, eying my trembling lip and bleeding knee suspiciously. 'I nearly set the archers on you, you stupid boy. If it happens again, then this gate will stay shut and you can sleep out there with the wolves and wild men for all I care.'

I was too shaken to answer back. But his words stung and I felt the red blood of shame rush to my cheeks as I crossed the long street between the barrack blocks.

He'd never have talked to me like that if my father was still here, I thought, resentment curling my hands into useless fists. *If he doesn't come home soon, they'll declare him dead and I'll be thrown out of here to fend for myself beyond the wall.* The thought of being all on my own in the wilderness, without family or friends or the protection of the soldiers, scared me even more than the thought of the waking stones following me through the night.

It wasn't like this for the other boys and girls the ordinary soldiers had with common women of the island. Only the centurions and those ranked above them could officially marry. But the other soldiers' unofficial local wives from the conquered lands to the south were also considered Roman citizens now. Their sons were trained for the army, their daughters working in the settlements that sprung up around the forts and conquered towns. Everyone was accepted, woven into the rich tapestry of Roman life that spread from the Mediterranean Sea all the way up to the outpost of the empire here at the Antonine Wall. Everyone except me. Even though my father was a high-ranking officer, I wasn't born of a conquered woman of the empire. I was born of a Damnonii, a wild and undefeated race the Roman army hadn't managed to subdue. I was an outsider, one of the enemy. Now that my father was gone, I was made to feel it more than ever.

I stopped below a sentry tower, warming my chilled hands at a brazier the guards on duty had set up to keep the autumn frost at bay. I couldn't hear them stomping back and forth across the boards above me as the noise from the kitchen block was overwhelming, but just knowing they were there and on the lookout was a comfort.

The stone giants won't dare climb the wall and cross into Roman territory, I told myself. *I'm safe as long as I'm here in the fort.* I could only hope if I repeated it enough times, I could make it true.

'What in the name of Jupiter is all that racket about?' Septicus Strabo, the legion's Standard Bearer, set down the pole with the bronze eagle he'd been polishing and grabbed hold of a passing kitchen slave. 'What's going on in there?' He pointed at the bustling kitchens by the officers' block. 'Has that idiot cook set the place on fire again?'

'No, sir,' the slave replied in halting Latin. 'It's the prepar– the prepara– the makings for the... the feast, see?'

'Feast? Who's having a feast? I wasn't invited to any feast.' Strabo shook the slave by the shoulders as though he thought he could jerk the answer out of him. Our legion's Standard Bearer was every bit as much a bully as Brutus. I hated him for the part he played in Bram's accident, and I had to bite my tongue every day to stop myself from telling him so.

'Nor are you likely to be, sir,' a legionary came to the slave's rescue before he was rattled to death. 'It's our second-in-command's idea. He invited some of the fancy folk from the Castlecary fort out east over for a banquet. "Change of scene", he said. If you ask me, old Taurus is looking ahead to the promotion once our Legate retires, if you catch my meaning?'

A group of three soldiers stopped by the brazier to heat their hands, squashing me back against the guard tower like they didn't even see me.

'When's our Legate coming back anyway? If he stays away any longer, Taurus will have the whole of our winter rations served up at his dinner table before any of us men get a bite of them,' one of the legionaries grumbled.

'He's still out west at the New Kilpatrick fort subduing the uprising with the other half of our legion,' Strabo sighed, picking up the eagle standard again and going back to polishing. 'Jupiter knows how long that'll take. Those wild tribe folk fight more like beasts than men.'

'Wish I'd been posted to New Kilpatrick instead of wasting my time here,' the first legionary muttered. 'All I've done for the last two years is dig latrines and go through my weapons drill till I'm marching in my sleep. Haven't had a good fight in so long, I've almost forgotten what blood smells like. A battle with the northern tribe folk would do us all good.'

'Yeah,' the other legionaries agreed. 'It'd wake us up, at least.'

'Don't get cocky,' Strabo warned. 'Those northmen aren't like anyone you've ever fought before. You weren't here sixteeen years ago when we laid the foundations for the wall. I was. Lost too many good men back then to count. They're not just wild, they're cunning, and vicious too. Those barbarians have no honour. They'll slit your throat in your sleep and wear your guts as a necklace if you don't stay wide awake. Trust me, boy, you don't want to fight the Damnonii for fun.'

'I don't want to break bread with them neither, but Lucius Aquila went and had a brat with one of them wild women and now we're stuck with that boy lurking round the fort like a bad smell.'

I tensed at the mention of my father's name. I was pretty sure the legionary knew I was standing right behind him, but he went on all the same.

'What was our Camp Prefect thinking, bringing that

tribe woman south of the wall? You'd have thought her stench was sweet perfume the way he looked at her. Remember when–'

'I'll not have a word said against Titus Lucius Aquila!' Strabo growled. 'He was Senior Centurion and my commanding officer long before you were even sucking your mother's milk, boy!'

The legionaries went quiet for a long moment, cowed by the Standard Bearer's rebuke. Then slowly, one by one, they turned to glare at me.

'What you looking at, tribe boy?' the first legionary snapped. 'Spying for your friends in the north, are you?'

'I don't have any friends in the north,' I answered truthfully. *Not after Bram's accident*, I added to myself. Out loud, I said, 'I'm a Roman, same as you.'

'Hear that, lads? The tribe brat thinks he's a citizen of the empire!'

'Might as well put a collar on a duck and call it a hunting dog,' the second legionary snorted.

'I've been trained to fight by my father!' I protested, my voice sounding shrill in the firelight. 'I'm going to join the army when I'm old enough and fight for Rome, same as you.' I tried to puff my chest out and stand tall like I'd seen the centurions do on the parade ground, but I felt small and weak beside the gleaming metal of the soldiers' armour.

'Any of you lads want to fight beside a tribe boy?' the first legionary laughed.

'Uh-uh.'

'Not me. Little traitor'd have my throat slit from behind if I took my eyes off him for even a moment in the file.'

'My father would have you whipped for speaking to me like that!' I squeaked, my voice giving away just how nervous I was. 'I'm the son of the Camp Prefect!'

'Former Camp Prefect. Your father's dead, boy. And if you talk back to anyone in this fort like that again, you'll be dead too.' Strabo said it so quietly I had to blink twice before I realised what he'd said.

'Marcus Lucius Aquila Felix, where in Jupiter's name have you been!' another much louder voice called from the officers' kitchen block.

If I'd thought it was a rescue, I was dead wrong. It was another ambush. The Quartermaster came storming out of the provisions store and headed my way with a face crimson with fury. 'I've been run ragged all afternoon trying to scrounge up supplies for this infernal feast, and I don't have time to chase lazy errand boys up and down the length and breadth of this god-forsaken island to ensure they get their jobs done. Where are those berries I sent you for hours ago?'

'Um...'

Capito had clearly told the Quartermaster he'd palmed his errand off on me. There was no way the flabby-bellied little man was going to complain to Brutus about it. Instead, I'd get all the blame. My hands had gone from chilled to sweaty in the space of a few moments, and I stuck them in my pockets so my trembling fingers wouldn't be on full view as I tried to come up with an excuse.

'They, um... there weren't any!' I blurted out. 'I scoured the hillside, I really did, but the bushes were stripped bare.'

'There were plenty left just two days ago when I sent a kitchen boy up the hill for relish,' the Quartermaster glowered at me. 'Are you telling me they magically disappeared overnight?'

'No, they must've been picked by the tribe folk. It's their hill, after all.'

There was a sudden intake of breath from every soldier within ten yards of me.

'Their hill?' The decurion got to his feet slowly, staring at me in disbelief.

'I mean, it's on their side of the wall, where they can reach it. Not that it's theirs. This land belongs to us. Us Romans. That's what I mean' I garbled.

Strabo took a menacing step towards me, but luckily for me the Quartermaster was too short-staffed to have one of his errand boys flattened when he had a feast to prepare.

'Come here, you little brat!' he snapped, grabbing me round the back of the neck and propelling me towards the kitchen. 'Our Legate's taken most of our slaves with him to the New Kilpatrick fort, and I can't run a banquet with the dregs of humanity he's left. If you can't do the one simple job I gave you, then you can thundering-well do another!'

The suspicious eyes of the Standard Bearer and the legionaries followed me all the way to the safety of the kitchen. I barely had time to let out the shaky breath I'd been holding when the Quartermaster passed me off to a man even more red in the face than he was. 'Here, Rufus, I've found you another pair of hands for the banquet.'

The head cook glanced up from the pots steaming over the roaring fire for the brief moment it took to look me up and down. 'He'll do. Cupbearer, come over here and show the boy what dishes he's to take in.'

One of the kitchen slaves hurried over and began piling

bowls of mutton and cabbage into my arms. 'Don't drop anything,' he whispered in my ear, 'or I'll get the blame.'

'Wait!' I spluttered, 'I'm not a slave! I don't serve at table!'

'You'll serve at table if I tell you to serve, tribe boy,' the cook growled. 'Now get those dishes over to the dining room before they go cold. Cupbearer, show him where to set them and make sure he doesn't spill anything over any of the nobles or I'll have you both whipped.'

I followed the kitchen slave meekly through the hall, my cheeks burning so bright with shame I could feel sweat beading my face. When my father was here, I was the son of the Camp Prefect – an officer's son – and that made me a scholar at the schoolhouse and a soldier in training. When he left, I was just a half-Roman, an errand boy who everyone looked sideways at in suspicion.

Now my father was a week or two at most from being officially declared dead, and I was being treated as a slave.

Things could not get any worse. Could they?

Chapter Seven

Jinny

I stared open-mouthed at the sight of my wee brother coming out of the mist, my heart half dying in my chest with fright. My aching jaw were what prompted me to speak at last, and when I found my voice again, the words that came out weren't kind ones.

'Bram, you wee nuisance! What in the name of the four winds are you doing creeping up on me like that? I were almost laid out cold with the fear!'

Bram laughed so hard at that he almost fell off the tiny pony he were riding. 'You should see your face, Jin! Looks like a pan of milk left to curdle for too long!'

'Least my face don't look like a mashed up–' I started to snap back, then bit my tongue to stop the cruel words from slipping out. Bram couldn't help the way he looked now. It weren't his fault. His bright wee face were crisscrossed with scars that split his cheeks in two and cut a great gouge from his chin to the ear missing on his left side. That weren't all he were missing. The spikes that tore great chunks of flesh from his poor thin body and left one arm hanging useless by his side had taken more than just a few lumps of meat out of him. His right leg were gone above the knee, his breeches sewn up to cover the stump of what were left.

They said he were lucky, Ailsa and all the rest of them. They said it were a miracle he'd survived at all after the healer sawed what were left of his mangled leg off. Even with her best balms and herbs made up into poultices, he bled for three days straight and coughed up twice his weight in bile. I near cried myself to death over him. I still cried at night over what he'd lost, and I knew he did too. But he never gave in to the sorrow, my wee Bram didn't. He'd get up each morning with a smile and pull himself up onto the pint-sized horse our pa traded half our worldly goods to get him, and trotted off looking for adventure just like he used to.

Tramper, the wee barrel-chested pony, didn't make up for Bram's missing leg, and she didn't make up for the dog I'd lost neither. But she were a gentle, patient wee thing, and I were glad for the way she clung to Bram the way Raggy had clung to me for the four springs he'd been mine till the accident. See, it were my Raggy that died in the spike pits that day, not Bram. It were his dead eyes that had looked up at me when I stared into the pit, and his death that the Roman boy were responsible for. I missed my dog so much it brought tears to my eyes to think of him. But I still had my Bram, and broken or not, I said a silent prayer of thanks to the four winds every night for saving his life.

'Did Ma send you looking for me?' I changed the subject quick as a flash afore he twigged I were about to say something mean about his face. 'Is she in a temper over the turnips?'

'Ma? No, it's our pa who wants you. You were meant to help him dig the back field to hunt the late kale stalks, 'member? Ach, Jin! You got a head like a leaky bucket for chores.'

'Just you wait till you're old enough to be sent hither and thither all day long to fetch this and carry that!' I shot back. 'Then you'll know all about it, Bram, my lad!'

Bram grinned at me and turned his horse to head back to the village. But it were a hollow smile, and I could see right through it to the ache beneath. Bram would never be able to do chores like the rest of us, no even a bairn's share never mind a man's when he were of age. It were one of the silent understandings between us, just like we never talked on how I were still a bairn running chores for the grown-ups instead of a woman. Some things were best left unsaid.

We walked in silence for a while, him on his wee pony and me on my tired feet, till Bram got to noticing how I kept looking back towards the valley. The sun had nigh on set behind the brae, and the band of mist between the slopes were swallowed up in the deeper dark of creeping night. I shivered in the growing cold, every shadow making me jump like a startled rabbit.

'What you looking at, Jinny?' Bram asked, seeing my face grow pale as the climbing moon. 'You see something behind us?'

'Nah, just keeping an eye out for metal men,' I lied, pulling my knife out of my pocket and showing him the sharp blade. 'Haven't had no chance to poke holes in one for longer than I care to remember.'

'You never poked holes in no metal man your whole life, Jin,' Bram laughed. 'And I'll bet a winter's worth of bread and dripping you wouldn't do it neither, even if you got the chance.'

'I'll no see you go hungry by taking that bet, Bram,' I smiled. But it were a cold smile, a guilty smile. A smile that twisted the corners of my mouth and tied great knots that writhed and squirmed right through me all the way down to my guts. He were wrong, see. For all his joking about my temper, Bram thought I were too good to hurt no one who didn't come asking for it. But I knew better. I knew what I'd done in the stone circle, what I were going to do to that Roman boy. It weren't my goodness nor forgiveness that had saved him from a blow to the head and a shock to the heart. It were sheer blind luck and my bad aim.

'You sure it's just metal men you're spying out for?' Bram asked again. 'You're looking awful pale, Jin.'

'I've no had any lunch, have I?' I snapped, quickening my pace. 'Been sent to both ends of the blessed earth running errands for every man, woman and bairn in the village today, I have.'

I should have told Bram there and then what I'd done. Before the accident, before his wee body were broken beyond repair, I would've come straight out and shared my secret with him without a moment's hesitation. But no now. Now he had enough trouble to deal with, what with his missing leg and the stares of pity from the other folk in our tribe. I wouldn't heap the weight of my sins on his pile of burdens for all the world.

My sins were chasing me through the dark, I were sure of it. Every time I turned my head, I saw shapes in the gathering night behind me. I'd woken the sleeping giants and now the great stones had climbed out of the valley and were crossing the grasslands behind us as swift and sure as silent demons. When I tried to fix my gaze on them and get a sense if they were real, they just melted back into the dark, and I were left straining my eyes in the dusk light, wondering if I'd gone half mad with terror.

'Come on, Bram, I'll race you!' My heart were pounding

too hard to stand the fear, and I couldn't fight the urge to run no more. 'Last one to the gate's a rotten egg!'

Bram were sporting enough to give me a head start afore setting Tramper to a canter that took him the length of two whole fields ahead of me. I didn't care about coming last, just as long as my wee Bram were safe behind the wooden fence that circled our village and kept the wild animals out. I could only hope it would do the job just as well for the wicked stone giants coming for me.

The gates were still open for the farmers and herders coming home from the fields, and I had to fight with myself to keep from shutting them and locking the latch pole in place. I'd got more than enough explaining to do for my lateness as things already stood without 'fessing up to waking the sacred stones and setting them to walking the grasslands round our village.

'You're a rotten egg, Jinny!' Bram crowed, trotting round me and tugging my hair. 'Poo! You're stinking up the whole village!'

The other bairns joined in till I were sick of the sound of chanting and ready to slap the next wee hand that reached for my hair. Bram were just in high spirits now that he'd mastered Tramper's paces after many new moons of hard practise, and the other bairns were looking for a distraction from their hungry bellies while they waited for the dusk meal. But I were in no mood to humour them tonight. I were heartsick with fear over the stones, and the bairns' laughter were another reminder that I weren't no woman of the village, just a daft wee lass who'd messed up yet again and proved why she weren't fit to be affirmed.

'That's enough!' I yelled, lashing out at a wee lad who

pulled my hair too hard. 'Get away with you all!' I hit the bairn harder round the head than I meant to, and he went tumbling to the dirt with a great red mark across his cheek. It weren't more than two moments later when he started howling, and that brought Ailsa and a couple of other women running from the milking shed.

'What have you gone and done now, Jinny?' Ailsa tutted, setting the lad to rights and rubbing his cheek with her apron. 'A great lump of a lass like you ought to know when to keep her hands to herself by now.'

'None of these wee brats would lift a hand to me in the first place if I'd been made a woman!' I protested. 'It's no fair, Ailsa! They treat me like I'm a wee bairn too!'

'And you act like one, Jinny, so you deserve it!' Ailsa shot right back. 'Where's them brambles I sent you for an age ago, hmm? What have you done with them?'

The brambles! Blast them to the four winds. In my hurry to run from the stone giants I'd clean forgot. 'Um...'

'You've been shirking off chores again, you lazy wee mop, haven't you?'

'I haven't, Ailsa, honest! I spent near enough the whole day scouring the bushes on the brae.'

'So where's the brambles to show for it then, hmm? And while we're about it, where's my basket?'

My head were so full of fear and confusion, I said the first thing that tickled my tongue. 'It were that Roman boy!' I lied. 'He jumped me on the brae and made off with my basket like the sneaking thief he is! More than that; he stripped all the rest of the bushes and made off with every last bramble to be found.'

'Ooh, he's a bad 'un that lad,' one of the mothers sighed,

and the other woman nodded like she believed me. Not Ailsa, though. Her scowl only dug ten feet deeper into her brow. It weren't her suspicious look that cut me, though. I were more than used to it by now. It were the look Bram threw me, like he couldn't figure out why I were telling mistruths about a boy he'd once counted as his best friend.

'Felix wouldn't do that, Jinny,' he said softly like he were disappointed in me. 'I know him. He wouldn't hurt no one. Not on purpose.'

'Wouldn't he now?' I spluttered, grabbing the empty cloth at Bram's leg stump and giving it a shake. 'What do you call this then, huh? What d'you call it if it's no the hurt that wicked boy caused?'

'Felix didn't do that, Jinny. It were the Romans who did that.'

'Felix IS a Roman, you daft wee turnip head!'

'He's no! No altogether! His ma were a Damnonii, same as us. That makes him almost kin. He were my friend, Jinny, and he were kind to me.' Bram's eyes were bright in the moonlight, and I could see he were close to tears. I should've dropped the matter there and then, but as usual, my head were too hot to keep a lid on my temper.

'That Roman boy were the one who sent you into that spike pit, and he's the reason you can't do more than drag yourself about with one good arm and a missing leg!' I yelled. 'If he hadn't gone and blabbed your secret, your face wouldn't be all mashed up and ugly and we could have a proper race across the fields instead of you pretending on that stupid wee spit of a pony!'

Bram took in a shuddery breath, then held it for a long moment while a big tear streaked down the remains of his face. I couldn't have felt worse if he'd gone and stabbed me in the heart with a red-hot poker.

'Ach, Bram, look, I didn't mean–'

'Let it be, Jinny. You've caused enough mischief for one day with your lies and laziness.'

It weren't Bram nor Ailsa who said that, it were our pa. He came up behind us all quiet-like and lifted Bram off the horse, setting him on his broad shoulders like he weighed no more than a half sack of turnips. 'Tie Tramper up in the barn and make sure she gets some fresh straw, Jinny,' he told me, heading for our hut without looking back. 'And apologise to Ailsa while you're at it, my lass.'

'Sorry, Ailsa, I'll try harder next time,' I mumbled, knowing it were only the first in a long string of apologies I'd be making that evening.

Ailsa sighed like she knew I didn't mean it, and the women went back to their milking. The bairns drifted off to their huts, following the scent of cooking smoke, and I were left standing all alone holding Tramper's reins and wondering why I couldn't never get a single thing right no matter how hard I tried.

I walked Bram's pony to the barn with my head hung low and my heart in my boots. The wind picked up in the darkness, whirling straw off the hay bales and whistling though the gaps in the fence posts. I put my eye to one of the gaps, peering out into the night and straining to see if the stone giants had made it as far as the fields. But it were no use. The moon were hidden by clouds and the shadows played tricks in the absence of starlight.

I knew they were there, though, the stones, standing somewhere just beyond the reach of my sight.

Silent.
Watching.
Waiting.

Chapter Eight

Felix

'Careful, you stupid boy! I want to eat that cabbage dish, not wear it!'

'Sorry, sir.'

I moved the bowl of pickled vegetables I'd placed too close to the edge of the table and mopped the patch of spilled vinegar with a cloth. I'd been trying to keep my head down as I shuttled between the kitchen and the huge dining room where the second-in-command and his family entertained his private guests, hoping I could get through the evening without drawing any more attention to myself. But now Taurus fixed his eyes on me, heaving his round belly up in his chair so he could grab my arm.

'I say, boy, stop a moment. Haven't I seen you somewhere before?'

He was looking at me, but the question was aimed at the officers sitting round the table with their wives and children. Slaves were never supposed to answer back. They weren't important enough to have anything to say.

'That's Titus Lucius Aquila's boy, sir,' Brutus said, his voice thick with too much wine. 'The tribe brat the former Camp Prefect had with a Damnonii woman. The one who caused all that trouble over the injured tribe boy last spring.'

'Ugh.' Taurus dropped my arm like he just found out he'd been holding a slug. 'What's he doing serving at table? Shouldn't he be at school or in the training corps or something?'

'He should be north of the wall with the other wild beasts, that's where he should be, sir,' Brutus grunted.

I bit my lip angrily but couldn't risk scowling at him openly. Not here in a room full of nobles where I was no better than a slave boy. By rights, Brutus shouldn't be here either, he was only an enlisted soldier, not a noble like the rest of the guests. Even my father had only ever been invited to sit at the Tribunes' table a couple of times in the last few years, and he was a full rank above Brutus. But the beetle-browed Senior Centurion had a way of worming into every command clique, whispering poisonous words laced with honey into the ears of the other officers. Taurus, the Tribune who was second-in-command of our second Augustan legion, had obviously fallen hard for his flattery.

'A real live tribe boy of the north!' One of the guests clapped her hands in delight. 'Oh, how wonderful! Come here, boy, so I can have a good look at you.'

I set the cloth down reluctantly and limped over to the other side of the table, my cheeks burning at the sudden attention. Taurus had invited several of the Tribunes and their wives from the eastern Castlecary fort for the banquet, and they all stared as though they expected me to turn into a wildcat at any moment and tear lumps from the furniture.

'Yes, he has the look of the north about him, a certain narrowness of the eyes and flaring of the nostrils, don't you think?' the noblewoman said, grabbing my face and turning it from side to side roughly as though I were a lump of meat on a butcher's slab.

'I don't see it at all,' another of the wives tutted, looking me up and down in obvious disappointment. 'He seems perfectly ordinary to me. Just another common child these ignorant soldiers insist on having with local women. Why they can't wait until they retire and are allowed to take official wives is beyond me.'

'But don't you think he has a little something of the north wind about him, just a touch?' the first woman appealed to her husband. The visiting Tribune glanced at me, shrugged, then went back to his wine cup. 'Can't see anything remotely interesting about him. He hasn't even got red hair.'

'Yes, that is disappointing.' His wife looked disapprovingly at my close-cut black curls and let go of my face, searching for something else that would prove how tribe-like I was. I knew they were just bored and looking for a distraction from the monotony of fort life, but the close inspection made me feel like a horse being examined at a dealer's yard. I hung my head, hoping they'd find something else to amuse them before I died of shame. But before she could lose interest, the noblewoman discovered my injured knee and with it, a whole new topic to embarrass me with.

'Oh, look! He's hurt himself, poor thing,' she exclaimed, grabbing a cloth from a passing slave girl and dabbing at my knee. The cloth was the one I'd used to mop up the spilt vinegar, and I winced when it stung the cuts beneath my torn breeches. 'Really, Furius Taurus, it's simply too cruel making a boy serve at table in this condition,' she frowned at our Senior Tribune.

'Not my orders, my dear, I don't know what he's doing here in the first place. Why have we got an officer's boy doing a slave's work at table, Brutus, hmm?' Taurus looked to the lowest-ranking officer present to find an excuse. Brutus cleared his throat and toyed with his cup, thinking quickly of a way to shift the blame despite being halfway to drunk on the Senior Tribune's expensive wine.

'As you know, sir, we're short of slaves at the moment,' he blustered. 'Our Legate's taken the bulk of our slaves west to the New Kilpatrick fort, and our supply lines from the south have been under attack since the midland uprising. We're having... manpower issues when it comes to keeping the kitchens and laundry running. I'm sure the boy doesn't mind helping out at table, especially as he's not proved much use at anything else so far.'

Brutus glared at me, daring me to contradict him, but I was too busy gritting my teeth at the vinegar bath my knee was getting to do more than let out a squeak of protest.

'Good lad,' Taurus nodded, pleased at the thought that I'd volunteered for the honour of fetching his wine and finger bowls for him instead of being press-ganged into it.

'By Jupiter! Your second Augustan's in a bad way if you can't even get enough hands together for a little evening party without enlisting the officers' children to serve,' one of the visiting Tribunes sniffed. 'At Castlecary, our sixth legion has some of the finest Nubian slaves you'll ever see. Our Senior Tribune had his own household serving staff transported from Gaul to wait at his table, and as for the dancing girls the Prefect in Rome sent our Legate as a gift... Oh! Exquisite.'

'I'm sure if our legion hadn't been split in two to man this fort as well as New Kilpatrick, we'd have just as many pretty slaves to serve your *cena*,' Taurus said stiffly, glowering at his guests across the table.

'Of course, of course,' the visiting Tribune murmured, hiding the sneer on his face in his wine cup.

The temperature in the room dropped abruptly. Competition between the legions was fierce, and it wasn't just fought over battleground honours, favours from the Roman Senate and promotions. Everything from the polish on the soldiers' armour to the lavishness of the banquets the Tribunes threw for each other could be used to prove which legion was superior. By the look of the rich silks and sparkling jewels the women in the dining room had piled on, the Tribunes' wives took their role in the inter-legion contest very seriously indeed.

Brutus, sensing a conflict he could turn to his advantage, leaned across the table and said softly to Taurus, 'Not to worry sir, I have the slave problem well in hand. If you leave it all to me, I'll have it sorted out by the end of the week.'

'Will you, by Jupiter?' Taurus beamed. 'That would be splendid.'

'Then I have your full permission to act as I see fit in this matter?'

'By all means, Brutus, my man, by all means. You are our acting Camp Prefect, after all.'

Brutus grinned and shot me a look that told me whatever he was planning, I wasn't going to like it.

By the time the guests had finished their dessert and were yawning over the remains of the wine decanters, my knee was aching worse than ever, and I'd heard enough camp gossip to last me a lifetime. My battle wound may have got me pity from that Tribune's wife, but it wasn't enough to get me out of the washing up. Between scouring pots and scraping scraps into buckets for the hunting dogs, I was fit to drop by the time the head cook finally let me go.

I hadn't made it ten steps out of the kitchens before I ran head-first into Capito and his own band of army cadets in training. He'd clearly been waiting for me, polishing his hunting knife till it shone in the moonlight. He held it up as I tried to brush past, blocking my escape with the sharp blade.

'Not so fast, tribe boy. Where are you going in such a hurry?'

'What do you want, Capito? It's late.' My head was aching and my hands were so raw and sore I could barely even feel the pain from my knee anymore.

'In a rush to get to your bed, are you?' Capito sneered. 'Looks like the wild beasts of the north aren't as tough as they're made out to be.'

The other boys laughed and clapped Capito on the back like he'd said something funny. I just blinked at him dumbly, waiting to see if he'd get bored and go away if I didn't respond. He didn't. He just got annoyed.

'So you're a slave now, eh?' he said, grinning at the state of my raw hands. 'About time you were put in your proper place. Don't worry, you won't be lonely in the kitchens all by your little tribe-boy self, though. There'll be more of you before the week's out, my father says.'

'What's that supposed to mean?' I frowned.

Capito looked shifty, like he'd just given something away that he didn't mean to. The other boys exchanged glances and whispered to each other behind him, trying to work out what he meant without being brave enough to come straight out and ask.

'Never you mind.' Capito scowled at me. 'Say a word to anyone, and I'll slit your throat faster than you can draw a stinking Damnonii breath.'

He toyed with the blade of the knife, cutting a strip from his leather belt so I could see how sharp it was. I really wasn't in the mood for his threats, and I was just too tired to be as scared of him as I usually was.

'Maybe you should, Capito,' I sighed. 'At least then I wouldn't have to look at your ugly face anymore.'

'What did you say, tribe boy?' Capito's face went red with anger, and the other boys closed in behind him ready to beat me to a pulp. Before they could lay their fists on me, another hand cuffed me round the back of the head, sending me sprawling to the ground.

'What are you lot doing up at this hour? Get back to your tents right now before I have the lot of you whipped!' Brutus came stomping from the barrack block with a couple of burly legionaries in tow, stopping only to flatten me and wave his fists at the other boys. 'Get to bed, all of you, or you'll each get a taste of my belt.'

'Yes, Father.'

'Sorry, sir.'

'We're going, sir,' the boys grumbled, running off to the south end of the fort where the tents for the soldiers' wives and children were pitched.

'And don't let me catch you lurking about after dark again,' Brutus called after them. 'I'll not have a bunch of kids wrecking the discipline of my fort by breaking curfew.'

It's not your fort, I thought angrily as I limped in the opposite direction from Capito and his gang. *My father's the*

Camp Prefect, not you. And when our Legate gets back from the New Kilpatrick fort, he'll make sure I spend my time in school instead of the kitchens. The commander of the second Augustan legion had always been kind to me despite being a nobleman, and I missed him almost as much as I missed my own father.

I should've gone straight to the tents with the other boys, but I wanted to wait till they were safely in bed before I ventured back for the night. Besides, there was something I had to check before I'd be able to sleep a wink. I crept to the base of the wall, careful to make sure the sentries on duty were far enough away to miss me in the dark.

Despite my weary limbs and aching knee, I pulled myself up the steep slope of turf to the walkway on top of the wall, peering out over the palisade into the darkness beyond. The moon was hidden behind thick clouds and I couldn't see all the way to the hill that hid the sacred valley. But I knew it was there, towering above the grasslands, looking down on all our misdeeds.

The silence of the night was broken by hushed voices at the gate, and I ducked down in the shadows, hoping no one could see me. There was a creaking of wood and hinges as the huge gates swung open, and the soft sound of leather boots on the bridge beyond.

That's strange, I thought. *No one's allowed out at night. Why would anyone want to go north of the wall at this time?*

I got back up and looked out over the palisade again, but I couldn't see anything moving in the darkness. Not soldiers, not tribe folk, and not the standing stones I was so afraid of. *Are they really awake?* I wondered. *Did Jinny really set the stone giants on me?*

I couldn't be sure. But one thing was certain. I was in

grave danger. It was only a matter of time before Jinny or the stones came to kill me.

The only question was: who would get there first?

Chapter Nine

Jinny

It weren't me they came for that night. It were Ailsa's son, Connor.

He were the head herder, always up at the crack of dawn to see to the cows long afore the rest of the village stirred. But no last night. He spent last night up in the wee hut on the other side of the Luggie River north of Tintock Brae, tending to a sick heifer with a wolf bite that were turning infected. If I'd known he were sleeping outside the safety of the village fence, up on the sheiling where the stones were walking the night, I'd have run out to warn him afore I curled up in my bedroll. I weren't about to admit to what I'd gone and done, but I'd have found a way to talk him into staying in the village till dawn; I know I would.

It were too late for that now. The stones had come for him in the dead of night, whisking him off to his doom and leaving nothing but an empty bedroll and the half-full pigskin bladder of cider the herders all kept with them to ward off the autumn chill. I knew that's all that were left of him, as it were me and Bram who were sent up the sheiling at first light to bring him his barley cakes wrapped in cloth with a hunk of cheese.

It were us who found the door to the hut hanging clean off its hinges like some huge hand had torn it open instead of knocking. It were us who found Connor's bedroll empty and the sick heifer missing. And it were us who found the dark smear of blood running down the doorpost. The blood mark were hand-shaped, like a man had clung to the doorframe to keep from being carried off into the night by evil spirits. Or stone giants.

'In the name of the four winds, Jin!' Bram gasped, nudging Tramper to the broken door of the wee hut and peering inside. 'Something uncanny's come to pass here, that's for sure! You think kelpies came up out the Luggie and dragged him off with them?'

'Don't be a deadwit, Bram, the Luggie's too wee a stretch of water for kelpies, they only live in the lochs of the north,' I snorted. I were a lot less calm than I sounded, though, and my hands shook as I fingered the gash of blood that clawed a great stain down the doorpost. I knew what had come to pass here last night alright, and it were a lot more uncanny than even Bram's wildest dreams.

'What should we do?' Bram gazed out across the sheiling for signs of life, but it were still too early for the shepherds to have come up with the sheep yet. 'Should we look for him?'

The thought of my wee brother wandering about in the pale half-light of dawn when the stones might still be walking abroad were what made my mind straight up. 'No, whatever took him is no something you and me can face down on our own, Bram. Run and fetch Ailsa and Pa, and make sure the village chief hears of this. Quick now!' I urged when he hesitated, his lip trembling at the thought of leaving me in that place of unknown mischief on my own. 'You'll go twice as fast as me on your horse. Go on now! You'll be back afore you know it.'

'Alright, Jin, but don't go anywhere till I get back with the big folk, you hear? And if any evil spirits come calling your name in the mist, don't answer them, promise?'

'I'm no daft, Bram! I promise.'

Bram didn't look too sure that I weren't stupid enough to give myself away if the nixies of the marsh came hunting, but he did what he were told, turning Tramper round and riding off for the village like his wee pony's feet were on fire. Despite my skin being so cold with fear I couldn't hardly feel my fingers nor my toes, it warmed my heart to see how sure he could handle himself in the saddle now.

It were almost a full new moon after the accident afore Bram had the strength to even sit up all by himself, and many new moons afore he could drag himself from one side of our hut to the other with his one good hand. When Pa piled all of our spare blankets, pots and farming tools into a barrow and set off to the market with our one goat and six of our eight chickens, I thought he'd gone mad with grief and were going to buy up all the cider north of the wall to drown his sorrows in. When he came back with that wee spit of a pony in their place, though, I didn't know whether to laugh or cry with relief. It took Bram an age to master the saddle and reins, but he never gave up, no even after falling and cracking his head on the ground for the hundredth time when his useless hand slipped through the reins, or his leg stump missed its grip going into a canter. Every day he got a wee bit more confident, and every day his smile got a wee bit brighter.

Look at him now, I thought, watching Tramper's white tail disappear across the sheiling. *If you saw him from a distance, you'd never know there were anything amiss with him.*

Sometimes I thought I were the one that were broken beyond repair when Bram fell into that pit full of spikes.

My heart smashed into pieces just like his wee body, but while Bram's wounds had healed, mine still festered red and sore as the first day I were cut. Maybe it were on account of losing Raggy. He were more than just my dog; he were my shadow, my best friend in all the world. He were a part of me, and without him, I couldn't put the broken pieces back together and stitch them up so they could heal, since there were a great big piece missing from the middle of my being. And every time I looked at Bram and saw his struggles and thought on how he used to run as fast as a spring hare, it were like a rusty nail were picking at the scab inside me, pulling the tender pieces apart again and making me bleed on the inside. But it weren't blood that came bubbling up from the wound inside me, it were raw anger. Ach, spirits of the four winds save me, I were so angry sometimes I couldn't hardly breathe with the strain of forcing it back down.

If I'd just got even with that poxy wee Roman boy I'd have room in my head to think straight! I growled to myself, trying to use the anger to drown out the fear that sat at the edge of my mind, waiting for the chance to take me over. *If I'd just smashed his stupid skull in and got done with it, I'd have justice for Bram and Raggy and I'd finally heal up all the hurt and get to sleep at night without such a cursed struggle.*

I leaned back against the wall of the hut, looking up the grassy rise that formed the head of the valley on the north side of Tintock Brae. The morning sun were up and yawning now. The autumn mist were already burnt clear off the hillside, running away to hide down in the sacred valley where the stones were standing watch. Thick fingers of fog curled into claws at the mouth of the valley pass, warning me back from the circle of giants lurking just out of sight behind the grey curtain. But I weren't stupid enough to go back in there never again.

Keep calm, Jinny, I told myself. *The stones only go walking at night, you're safe now.*

The thought didn't go much ways to soothing me. I might be out of danger till next nightfall, but Conner were took and eaten, and it were all my fault. The giants were awake, and they'd come walking again tonight, and the next night, and the next, taking us all one by one till they were full and went back to sleep again. Anyone else they carried off in the dark would be on my conscience too.

Should I tell? I wondered, shielding my eyes against the bright rays of dawn to watch for Bram coming back from the village. *Should I just 'fess up to what I've gone and done and take the punishment?*

I knew it were only the right thing to do. But I couldn't stomach the thought of being up afore the Council again, proving how right they were to keep me from the Bairntime's Passing ceremony. I'd be a wee lassie my whole life in the eyes my tribe, and I couldn't bear that no more than I could bear Pa's disappointment nor Ma's sorrow. All I could do were hold my tongue for the time being till I puzzled out a way to send the stones back to sleep.

Bram and Tramper were trotting into view now, a crowd of village folk gathered behind like a string of geese on market day. When they got up close and I saw Ailsa's face sick with worry as she were carried by Pa and our village chief, my guts twisted with guilt and I could scarce find my voice to answer their questions.

'You've no touched anything inside, lass, it's all just the

way you found it?' Gregor asked when he'd looked inside the wee hut. I nodded, not trusting myself to meet his eye. I'd spoke no more than ten words altogether to our village chief since the night of the accident, and none of them had been offered willingly.

'You think it's the Maeatae?' one of the other herders asked, looking north to the Camsith Fells. Raiding parties from beyond the high hills were rare as snow in summer, but it weren't impossible.

Gregor shook his head. 'They'd come for the cattle or the sheep, they'd no settle for one sick heifer and a herdsman. And they'd no carry Connor off with them either, they'd just...' He trailed off, seeing Ailsa's face turn pale as death when she caught his meaning.

'Maybe they hid the proof of their deeds nearby,' Pa said, fingering the smear of blood on the doorpost. 'We should split up and look.'

It were a fair suggestion, but it sent shivers down my spine none the less, more so on account of it coming from Pa. He weren't the same since Bram's accident. He were always hopeful afore, always ready to think the best of people and trust that things gone awry would turn out well in the end. Now there were a darkness in his eyes that never seemed to clear with the dawn, and I were heartsick at the thought of the burden of hurt and crushed hopes he carried on account of his broken son. Bram saw it too and it cut him deeper even than it cut me. He couldn't bear the thought of Pa thinking less of him now that he were missing a leg and carrying a useless arm. Maybe that were why he'd worked twice as hard since the accident to stay cheerful and prove he were no worse off than he were afore.

'Don't worry, Ailsa, Connor's stronger than our black-smith's prize ox.' Bram squeezed Ailsa's hand and gave her a cheery smile. 'There's no way he's come to harm. That heifer probably ran off in the night and Connor's halfway up the furthest sheiling chasing him back.'

Ailsa nodded gratefully and sat down on a tree stump to wait for the searchers to come back with news, but I could tell from the way she eyed the bloodstain on the doorpost that she didn't think they'd bring her anything she wanted to hear. I fussed and fidgeted, wandering up and down the banks of the Luggie as though I were searching too. But my heart weren't in it. I knew where Connor had gone, and I knew he weren't never coming back.

When Pa and Gregor and the rest of the herders finally headed back to the hut, they had two riders with them. Bram saw them first coming east across the marsh, and he called me over to watch and hear him guess where they were from and what they were doing on our turf.

'Hush, lad, you'll hear soon enough,' Ailsa scolded, standing up and hobbling over to meet the returning group. When she got up close and her weak eyes made out that her son weren't with them, her shoulders slumped so low I thought she were going to collapse like an over-tall pile of autumn leaves. I hurried to her side to hold her steady, feeling like the worst traitor in all the world when she held my arm and smiled gratefully at me. I were the one causing her pain at the loss of her son, and here I were playing the part of a good wee lassie who only thought on others and their comfort. My mouth were so full of the bitter taste of self-disgust, I near choked myself hoarse. I swallowed the bile down, but it didn't help.

'Where are the men from, Gregor?' Ailsa asked. 'Have they got word of my son?'

'No one's seen him, Ailsa, but it's worse than that,' Gregor said, his face all lined with trouble. 'The riders are from Torrance and Kinkell. They're calling a meeting of the villages at the hallowed tree.'

'What in the name of the four winds for?' Ailsa gasped. Bram's eyes widened and my heart near jumped clean out of my mouth for fear that my misdeeds had been discovered by the rest of the tribe.

'Connor weren't the only one to go missing last night,' Pa said. 'Two shepherds from Kinkell and a lass from Torrance have vanished without a trace and all.'

'But how? Why?' The way Ailsa said it, it were more of a wail than a question.

'We don't know,' Gregor shook his head. 'But when the village Elders come together by the tree at midday, I swear by my beard we'll get to the bottom of this.'

It didn't matter that the sun were full up in the sky overhead now. My heart turned so cold in fear at his words that my whole body were gripped with a chill worse than winter.

They're going to find me out! I shuddered. *And when they do, they'll punish me even worse than last time.*

I almost wished they'd just find out now and be done with it so I didn't have to wait. The first blush of dawn had passed, but I had all the slow creep of time till midday to wonder with dread what that punishment might be.

Chapter Ten

Felix

'What are you doing sneaking about here, boy?' the legionary guarding the entrance to the officers' kitchen snapped. 'Get yourself to the schoolroom and stop looking for mischief!'

I blinked at him in surprise. I'd never seen a sentry on duty at the door before. Even the camp hangers-on in the tent town wouldn't risk stealing from the officers' kitchen. No one was that stupid.

'I'd much rather be in school,' I said, 'but the Quartermaster told me to report to him for duties this morning.'

The guard eyed me suspiciously. Between worrying about the stones Jinny had set on me and the possibility that even if I lived, I'd end my days as a slave instead of a soldier, I hadn't got much sleep last night. My eyes were red-rimmed and my hands were raw and swollen from scouring pots. Yesterday's kitchen chores meant that I hadn't time to visit the laundry block to wash my spare tunic, so the one I wore beneath my cloak still had stains of vinegar, beetroot relish and oyster sauce from my sloppy attempts at serving. I was looking less like an officer's son and more like a slave every day. I even smelled like a fishmonger had spilled a bucket of market dregs over me. No wonder the guard on duty was confused.

Just then, the Quartermaster came bustling out to clear up the question of my status.

'There you are, you lazy little toad! Been catching up

on your beauty sleep while the rest of us work, have you? Looks like a waste of time in your case.' He eyed me up and down with a snort, and the guard at the door smirked when he realised that I was just a lowly errand boy.

'Get yourself out the gate and up the hills. I need mushrooms for tonight's *cena* and they aren't going to pick themselves.'

'You mean north of the wall?' I asked, my heart beating faster at the thought of leaving the safety of the fort.

'Yes, north of the wall!' the Quartermaster growled. 'Where d'you think I meant? Mesopotamia? Get going!' I was used to getting baskets shoved at me by now, and I caught the one the Quartermaster swung my way before it could smack me in the stomach.

'But can't I go south? I mean, there's plenty of good mushroom patches near the drainage ditches,' I protested. I was pretty sure the stones hadn't made it over the wall last night. The alarm would've sounded the length and breadth of the Roman occupation line if a group of stone giants had come marching up the turf embankments. South of the wall was safe. North of the wall was asking for trouble.

'You're the only brat here who speaks that local tribe gibberish, so you go out the front gate for supplies whenever I tell you, understand?' The Quartermaster was dangerously close to losing his temper. From the bags under his eyes, he didn't look like he'd got much sleep last night either. That was odd. For the first time I noticed the shutters were closed along the windows of the officers' block, and the doors and windows of the prison house opposite were bolted shut. There was something going on in there that anyone under the rank of centurion was not supposed to see.

I didn't get the chance to work it out, though. One hard shove from the Quartermaster was enough to send me on my way, his parting orders ringing in my ears.

'And no dawdling this time! Get back as quick as you can – Cassius Brutus has a job for you to do this afternoon.'

Brutus has a job for me? What in the name of Jupiter can he want my help for? I thought as I headed for the gate. Whatever work the Senior Centurion had lined up for me, it was bound to be unpleasant. That was two mysteries in as many moments that I'd have to solve.

After a quick word to the sentries on duty, the great north gates swung open and I tramped my unwilling way over the bridge and onto the openlands beyond the safety of the wall.

It was a warmer day than we'd had for weeks; the sun was up and the sky was blue and cloudless. But there was a strange hush in the air, as though the birds were holding their breath and waiting for something dreadful to happen. I kept well clear of the hill that hid the sacred valley, hunting for mushrooms between the grass clumps beyond the *lilia* pits. Every time I straightened up, I saw the wisps of fog that curled up from behind the hill, and I thought with a shudder of the stone giants coming towards me one step at a time through the mist. If I stared too long, I was sure I could make out dark shapes moving just behind the grey veil in the distance. It gave me goosebumps being out on this side of the wall with no gate and palisades and no sentries standing between me and the stones in the valley.

I was pretty sure my mother said the stones only went walking at night if they were woken. But like so many of my memories of her, the story was broken and fragmented, a whirl of tiny pieces I struggled to put together. Whenever I tried to recall my mother's face or the way she laughed, it was like looking at a stone sinking underwater, the memories all rippled and spreading further apart the more time passed. I was terrified that one day I'd wake up and find I'd forgotten her entirely. It was worse now that my father was gone and I had no one to talk to about her.

Maybe he won't come back and I'll forget him too, I thought darkly. *Maybe instead of a soldier, I'll end up a slave in a foreign land – an outsider with no kin, like a boat that's been shorn of its anchor.* I didn't know whether it was that thought or the fear of the stones that made me shiver more.

It was no good. There were no mushrooms to be had this close to the wall. I'd have to head for the trees to stand a chance of filling the Quartermaster's basket and dodge a beating for disobedience. And that meant going deeper into enemy territory.

They're not my enemies, I tried to tell myself. *My mother was a Damnonii, and that makes me half tribe-born. I'm just going for a walk on my mother's lands, that's all.* It didn't make me feel any better as I made my way carefully towards the copse at the far end of the grassland. Especially as I spent most of my time trying to convince the other boys in the fort that I was every bit as Roman as they were.

I hadn't been back to the copse since the accident. I knew Brutus and some of the soldiers on sentry duty went there for rabbits, as I saw them coming back through the gate sometimes with the skinned bodies hanging from their belts. But I kept away whenever I was sent north of the wall. I didn't want to be reminded of what happened to Bram or Jinny's dog.

Despite my reluctance, the copse was almost as good a place for mushroom gathering as it was for hunting rabbits. The roots of the skeleton trees hid a whole forest of ripe fungus, and soon my basket was full of soft mushroom caps as big as serving bowls. I was just going to head straight back to the wall to deliver my load when I realised the midday sun was no longer warm on my face and the sky was hidden behind a thick belt of cloud. That was the way the weather was in this unpredictable land: one moment the sky would be smiling at you, the next it was dumping a latrine-load of rain right on your head with hardly a murmur of warning.

I'd been so busy picking that I hadn't noticed the fingers of mist stroking the trees on the outskirts of the copse. Now as I looked up and saw the fog line creeping towards me across the grass, my hand froze halfway to the last mushroom in the clump. I wasn't sure whether it was the wind stirring the branches, or the shadows of trees behind the curtain of fog, but it seemed as though something was moving in the mist towards me. Something dark and ominous with the tang of age and moss. Something that cut off my escape route south of the copse to the wall.

I wasn't about to wait and find out whether I was just imagining things. I ran, fleeing for the higher ground where the fingers of mist couldn't reach me. This time, I kept hold of my basket, mushrooms spilling out and rolling back down the slope as I headed for the high meadow where the hallowed tree of the Damnonii stood. When I cleared the rise and stumbled out from behind a screen of rock, I got such a surprise I nearly dropped the whole load of mushrooms in a heap.

I'd expected the meadow to be empty, with only a few specks of shepherds and herders on the pastures in the distance. They kept their sheep and cattle well away from the hallowed tree that rose in the centre of the Damnonii lands. But the field wasn't empty. By the looks of it, every tribe member from every village north of the wall had turned up to crowd into an enormous circle round the tree, some standing, some sitting and some trying to climb on the shoulders of others to get a better look.

I took a step back, ducking behind the outcrop of rock again before I was seen.

But it was too late.

'Hey, Felix! Come to spy on us?' A shadow blocked the light, and I turned to see a boy on a dirty white horse scowling down at me. His face was criss-crossed with scars, one empty trouser leg sewn up and strapped to the saddle so the remains of his thigh could grip the horse's flank on the right side. Only one hand held the reins, the other hanging oddly loose at his side. I looked down quickly, sick to my stomach at the sight of what the Roman spike pits had done to him.

'No, Bram, of course not. I've just been sent out to pick mushrooms. I didn't know your tribe had a meeting. I'm sorry, I didn't mean to see anything I shouldn't.' It came out in a mumbled rush, and I could feel my face turning hot despite the cold. I wasn't sure why I was so ashamed. Maybe it was the guilt I still felt at sharing his secret. Maybe it was seeing his injuries for the first time. Or maybe I felt bad I hadn't been allowed to visit him since the accident. The other Damnonii had made it clear I wasn't welcome anywhere near his village. All I knew was my guts were squirming and I wanted to be a hundred miles away at that moment.

'Don't go twisting yourself up, Roman boy, I were just jesting.'

I looked up again. It took me a moment to realise Bram wasn't scowling after all, it was just the way the scars met above his eyes that made him look like he was angry at first glance. But when I looked closer, I saw he had a broad smile on his face and his cheeks were dimpled with laughter.

'Sheesh-o-man! You've pulled up half the fairy houses in the wee folk's kingdom! They'll no thank you for that. You having a feast in that big fort of yours or something?'

I smiled back, and when I did it was like all the guilt and shame went melting off into the far distance, leaving me wondering how I could ever have thought Bram would blame me for the accident in the first place. That's just not the way he was made. He was like the sunshine: no matter how dark the clouds got, he always came out the other side with a warm smile on his face.

'How are you getting on, Bram? Are you alright?' I asked, trying not to stare at his sewn-up trouser leg. I was pretty sure he knew what I meant.

'No so bad.' Bram gave a contented nod like half his body wasn't either missing, useless or chewed up with scars. 'I got this wee pony to run about on now. "Tramper", she's called. What do you think?'

I patted the tiny horse on the neck and she turned to lunge at my basket, nearly tossing Bram clean out of the saddle. He pulled on her reins and gave her a kick with his good leg, settling her back down with a skill that must have cost him a great effort to master.

'She's a greedy wee maggot!' He laughed at my startled face. 'She got into the hay store the other day and near ate half the barley seed afore we got her back out. Sheesh! Jinny got a sore belting and no mistake for no tying her up right in the barn at sundown.'

I bent to pick up the spilled mushrooms, and there was silence between us for a long moment. The people hidden from view on the other side of the rock more than made up for it, though. It seemed like a thousand crows had come home to roost at once, all raising their voices in outcry and flapping to be heard in the din. I wanted more than anything to know what was going on, but before I could ask, there was something else that had to be said first.

'Look, Bram, I'm really sorry I told your secret to the other Romans. I didn't mean for any of the trouble to happen. I just wanted to... I mean... It was–'

'I know,' Bram shrugged like I'd said something that made sense instead of babbling. 'I can guess it's no easy for you, Felix, no being one of us, but no being near enough one of them that they'll overlook the tribe blood in you. And with your ma gone and your pa somewhere far away, well... ' He gave a long whistle, and left it at that.

I stared at him open-mouthed. Bram had only turned eleven in the summer, but he had a wiser head on him than half the senators in Rome.

'You mean... you don't blame me for...?' I nodded at his leg.

Bram shook his head. 'I did at first, and for a good bit after. But there's no sense blaming someone who didn't mean no more harm than trying to get on the good side of a bunch of bullies he has to live with. I'm no happy about you blabbing that secret, and I'll maybe no trust you for a wee bit longer, mind, but I'm no bitter at you no more, Felix.'

'Then we can still be friends?' I asked hopefully.

'I reckon so. You'll have to keep clear of Jinny, though. She's gone half crazy over the loss of her dog. She'll have your head on a spike at our village gate if she catches sight of you, so just you watch out!' He grinned when he said it like he thought it was a joke and his sister would never actually do something like that.

Then Jinny's not told him what happened in the stone circle yesterday, I thought. *Maybe it's just as well.*

'So, what's going on, Bram?' I said out loud. 'It's not your Samhain festival for a whole week yet. Why's everyone come together?'

'Oh, there's trouble brewing, and no mistake.' Bram's smile faded. 'But we'll no get to the bottom of it way back here. Got to get up to the front if we're to hear what the Elders are saying.'

'I can't go out there!' I protested. 'As far as the Damnonii are concerned, I'm as Roman as the rest of the soldiers! They'd slit my throat as soon as they set eyes on me!'

'Nah, you're just a half-tribe lad, they won't do you no harm. Here, stick this on you and no one'll see that great big Roman nose you got.'

Bram handed me his tartan cloak, and when I'd draped it over my shoulders and pulled up the hood, I was a bit more confident no one would look twice at me.

'You ready to hear what all the fuss is about?' Bram asked, patting his horse and turning her towards the crowd.

I hesitated for only a moment. I didn't want to go back down into the mist on my own just yet, not with the shadows walking about and the birds so strangely silent. And I had to admit, I was curious to hear what had gathered so many of the tribespeople together in one place. Whatever it was, I had a sinking feeling it wasn't something good.

'Lead the way, Bram,' I said. 'I'm right behind you.'

Chapter Eleven

Jinny

The Elders weren't coming together at the hallowed tree to find me guilty of waking the stone giants and causing them to go stomping about eating folk after all.

That were a relief and no mistake.

But what they had got together to talk about were just about as bad. Four villagers had gone missing last night – the two shepherds from Kinkell and the lass from Torrance had vanished without a trace, same as our Connor, and not a hair of them seen since sundown yesterday. The crowd of people were all jumpy and nervous thinking it were maybe a band of Maeatae come over the Camsith Fells who done it, or maybe a wild animal, the likes of which we'd no seen afore, were loose on the sheilings. That idea had the herders squawking like a clutch of plucked chickens setting eyes on the cooking pot.

'Silence! Everyone calm down!'

Our Gregor stood up and held up his hands. It took a while afore the folk in the crowd stopped their jabbering and settled down to hear him. Gregor weren't the senior tribe chief, but Morag from Torrance were so old her voice came out like a pair of wheezy bellows. She didn't stand no chance of being heard in a field of crickets never mind the rabble crowded round the hallowed tree. So it fell to Gregor with his voice like a thunderstorm to shut us all up and tell us what the Elders had stood there gabbing about.

'I know you're all fretting over the thought of Maeatae

raids, but since the peace treaty five seasons back, we've had no more trouble on that count. Some of the Kinkell herders have seen a pack of wolves roaming close by the sheilings, so we're sending a band of hunters out to bring home their skins and see if they can find traces of the missing villagers.'

Half the crowd nodded while the other half raised a great grumbling under their breath. Folks were never so happy as when they'd got something to complain about.

'But what if it's no the wolves?' one of the farmers from Torrance shouted. 'What if it's them cursed metal men that are up to no good?'

'What would the Romans want with a handful of villagers who can't even speak their babble of a language?' Gregor called back. 'That don't make no sense.'

The farmer were clearly one of them types who likes a quibble better than a dog that's found a hunk of bone to chew. He weren't about to let it drop without another gnaw at it. 'But what if it were something uncanny that took them? Something we've no means of fighting, like nixies or the wee fairy folk?'

I stood on the edge of the crowd with my ma and fidgeted like my skirts were made of stinging nettles. That farmer were digging around too close to my buried pot of guilt for me to breathe easy. *Spirits of the four winds, don't let any of them folk stumble onto the idea of the standing stones being wakened up!* I prayed like my life depended on it. *Let them think it's wolves for now till I can fix the mischief I've done.*

Lucky for me, the Elders had done with talking and wanted to see a bit of action. The farmer got his ear chewed out for being a prattling old fear-monger, and the crowd were told to go home and get on with their day till the hunters came back with news for them. Ailsa huffed and hummed at that, clearly no too happy at the decision.

'I know it's no quite what you were hoping for,' Ma said kindly, putting her hand on Ailsa's arm and trying to cheer her along. 'But the hunters are bound to come back with better news afore the sun goes down.'

'News, aye,' Ailsa sighed, 'but no my Connor, there's the pity of it.'

'Ailsa, why'd you no stand up along with the other Elders and say your piece to them?' Mairi-with-the-yellow-pigtails asked. 'It's no like you to be shy of your place.'

'When you're old enough to have a lick of sense, you'll know it's no good for the tribe when an Elder with a deal too much salt in her heart sticks her spoon in the cooking pot,' Ailsa said severely. It took Mairi a moment to work out she were being scolded, but Coira-as-tall-as-a-rowan-tree were quicker off the mark and jumped in to defend her daft wee sister.

'She didn't mean no harm, Ailsa. We're all worried about Connor, he's about as fine a lad that a lassie could wish to clap eyes on.'

'You've no been a woman more than five new moons and you're already making eyes at a lad with almost twice as many seasons under his belt?' Ailsa tutted. 'Spirits of the long night help us, what are the young folk coming to these days?'

Coira saw me grin at that, and her and her sister getting two scoldings in as many breaths were as much as she could take without handing me a share of them.

'I don't know what you're smirking about, Jinny,' she

snapped. 'It'll be a long while yet afore you're even woman enough to sit in the weaving shed never mind look at the lads of the village that way.'

It were a sideways blow, and one I'd no seen coming. Me and the four new-made women were thick as thieves afore Bram's accident, and it hurt worse than a scald from an over-cooked pan of porridge to be reminded that my age-mates no longer saw me as one of them.

'Look all you like, Coira,' I snapped back. 'With your ugly face, there's no a lad from here to the Highlands who'd do you the favour of looking your way in return.'

'Coira's a deal sight prettier than you, with your mop of hair so tangled you could sweep the floor with it!' Mairi chimed in, taking her sister's side in our quarrel. 'I don't know why you always have to say such mean things, Jinny! If they'd just chopped your tongue off last spring and had done with it, you'd be ready for womanhood along with the rest of us.'

'Aye,' Coira nodded. 'It's that wicked wee lick of flesh that'll keep you a bairn till the day you breathe your last.'

Afore I could prove her right, my ma grabbed my hand and squeezed hard, giving me her silent warning to shut my big mouth and no shame her in front of the rest of the tribe. I had to bite down awful hard to keep the words inside. By the time Mairi and Coira had met up with barrel-shaped Ethne and pretty-as-heather Rhona and gone walking back to the village with the other women, my mouth were filled with blood and my throat were sick with the taste of it.

'Well done, lass,' Ma whispered, giving me a wee peck on the head when no one was looking. 'I know that weren't easy for you.'

I swallowed hard, Ma's kindness helping me fight off the tears of resentment that were trying to force their way out. 'It's no fair, Ma!' I whined. 'I'm just as ready as them to be made a woman. Can you no speak to Gregor about it?'

'It's no up to me or your pa to decide,' Ma sighed. 'You'll just have to do your best to prove to everyone you're ready for the ceremony, Jinny, and that means keeping a lid on that temper of yours for starters.'

'My temper's no done anyone a lick of harm,' I muttered. 'I don't see why to be made a woman, I have to turn myself into a meek wee sheep. Anyhow, if I weren't full of fire, I'd die of cold when the winter set in.'

Even as I said it, I knew it weren't true. My temper were what got Connor and the Kinkell lass and the two shepherds taken away by the stones. I'd gone and woken them up with my thirst for revenge, and that were plenty harm enough for one lifetime. If I didn't come up with a way of sending them back to sleep soon, I'd have the guilt of more than the four missing villagers to keep me up at night.

'Ailsa, you know how the stories say the stones in the sacred valley need to be sung to sleep?' I began afore the old woman could go hobbling back home with the rest of them.

'What of it, Jinny?' Ailsa's eyes were narrowed like she thought I were going to dig my grandma's buried quarrel back up and beat her about the head with the yellow bones of it.

'Well, I were just wondering... Say one of them metal men stumbled into the valley and woke the stones by mistake,' I said slowly like I'd just thought of the idea there and then. 'How would one of us soothe them back to sleep again?'

'You've no seen the Romans go marching about in our sacred valley, have you, lass?' Ailsa gasped.

'No, no! Course not!' I tried to smile like it were a silly idea, but I reckon it just looked like I were sucking lemons. 'I mean, it's just imagining. One of them "just-in-case" kind of things you're always telling me to think on.'

'Thinking of fairy stories is for bairns, Jinny. It's the grown-up work of planning on storing grain and putting plenty of dry thatch by afore the rains that I were talking about.'

I frowned. We were dancing round my question in circles that were getting further and further away from the answer I were trying to fiddle out of Ailsa.

'Aye, I know,' I tried again. 'But just for the sake of imagining, say the metal men were to come stomping through the valley with their swords and spears. Say they were whistling and laughing and shouting up a storm without minding about the stone circle, and say–'

'Whistling?' Ailsa's eyes widened till her milky white one were as wide as the moon. 'Even the Romans would no be daft enough to go whistling down in the sacred valley.'

'How no?' My heart were already halfway to my boots afore I heard her answer.

'Why, whistling's the very thing that'll shake them wide awake and set them walking across the land at night looking for the one who woke them.'

'But Ailsa!' I wailed, trembling from head to toe now. 'My grandma said the stones could be kept asleep with the magic song. What did the Elders go and teach us the tune for when we were no bigger than knee-high if we weren't never to use it?'

'Aye, Jinny, your grandma were right on that score – singing's the very thing that keeps them slumbering. "Sing me a song, lass, lull me to sleep", that's the thing to remember around the stones.'

'And whistling?' I gulped.

'Do you no remember the words?' Ailsa frowned. "Hum me a tune, lad, whistle me home". That's what the stones want, see? To be woken with whistling and called home to the land of the living. If you ever see anyone near that valley doing anything but singing the song all quiet-like under their breath, you come running to tell me and I'll set them straight, understand?'

I nodded so hard to cover my lies my head near came off my neck.

'Right then, I've got better things to think on just now than fairy tales,' Ailsa said, grabbing two passing farm lads round the neck and bidding them carry her home between them. 'Mind you remember what I told you, lass!' she called back over her shoulder.

'Remember what, Jinny?' Pa asked, coming up behind me with that quiet way of his and near sending me jumping clear out my skin.

'To think on storing grain and putting plenty of dry thatch by afore the rains,' I rattled off to keep him from guessing at my wicked deeds. He gave me a searching look I were sure could see right through to the badness eating up my heart. Then he sighed and said, 'Leave the grain and thatch to me and your ma for now, lass. It's the back field that's been needing your notice since yesterday. There's a patch of late turnips mouldering there and a line of bushes still heavy with nuts on the spoil seeing as you've been turning your nose up at the work. Get it done, Jinny. Don't make me ask again.'

'I will, Pa, almost this moment,' I said.

'Almost?'

'I've just one wee thing to do first, then I'll be right there!'

I took off across the meadow, pushing my way past the last of the gossips and doom-mongers who'd stayed longer than the rest to swap their made-up stories of our tribe's coming troubles. 'Bram!' I shouted. 'Bram! Wait!'

I'd spotted my wee brother sitting near the front of the crowd on his pony earlier, but it weren't until folks started heading for home that I got to wondering who that other lad sitting up behind him wrapped in Bram's cloak were. He were too big for one of the bairns of the village, and the older lads weren't likely to hang around with a poor wee thing like Bram anyhow. They liked to stick with the older farmers and shepherds to show what big men they were even though some of them weren't no taller than me. I had a sneaky suspicion I knew who the hooded stranger might be, and it grew even sneakier when I saw Bram look over his shoulder, then nudge Tramper into a faster trot when he caught sight of me on her tail.

'One more step and I'll have the pair of you out of that saddle and flattened into oatcakes!' I snapped, jumping in front of the pony just as they rounded a big rock and looked set to go cantering down the slope to the copse.

'Aw, Jin, leave off, will you? We weren't doing no harm!'

Bram grumbled, trying to nose Tramper past me. I caught the reins and gave the wee pony such a smelly stink-eye that she didn't dare move another hoof till I gave her the say-so.

'If that great lump behind you means no harm, then what's he doing hiding his face like he's afeared someone's going to see him?' I demanded, tugging at the cloak the boy were trying to wrap tighter round himself. I knew who it were long afore I got the best of the tug-o-war game and the cloak came sliding off. The Roman boy sat there blinking at me with a sheepish look on his face like he were sure I'd never have figured it out if only he'd kept a tighter grip of the tartan.

'You've got some nerve showing your ugly face round here after what you've done!' I growled, ready to pull him clean off the horse and send him rolling down the hill to the copse where he'd caused all the trouble.

'He's only showing his face 'cause you went and unhooded him, Jin,' Bram said. 'Can't you give up on blaming him for everything? Aw, come on, Jinny, it's been an overlong time and I'm dying for us all to be friends and forget what can't be helped.'

'Forget?' I near choked myself on the word.

'Yes, Jinny, forget.' It were the Roman boy who spoke up. He had a funny look on his face now, like he weren't scared of me no more. 'If you can forget the mistake I made telling the soldiers about the rabbits in the copse, then I can forget all about what you did yesterday. Is it a deal?'

The Roman boy's words chilled me to the bone.

'What do you mean by that, Felix?' Bram turned round in the saddle to look at him, then back at me. 'What did you do yesterday, Jinny?'

'Nothing,' I snapped. 'I didn't do nothing yesterday. Don't you go listening to no more of this wicked boy's lies, Bram.'

'But-'

'There's nothing to tell, Bram, really, I was just joking. That's what friends do, right Jinny?' Felix looked me square in the eye like he were asking me silently whether we had a deal or not.

'I guess so,' I shrugged, fizzing with anger at the way he'd got the better of me and there weren't a thing I could do about it. There weren't no way I wanted Bram knowing I'd near knocked that Roman boy's head off with a rock and woken the stone giants into the bargain.

'So we can all be friends then?' Bram looked fit to celebrate all the birth seasons of his lifetime all at once.

''Course, Bram, there's nothing I'd no do for you,' I said, throwing that Roman boy a warning look. 'Nothing.'

'That's just grand! Come on, Jin, race you to the copse.'

'I got to go turn over the back field,' I told him, itching to get away from that Roman boy and his smug smile. 'Keep well away from the wall, you hear? And don't take Tramper nowhere near the sacred valley.'

'I'm no daft, Jin!' Bram laughed as he trotted off down the slope with the Roman boy bouncing along behind him.

'Mind you're back at the village afore it gets dark!' I yelled.

I could only hope he heard me.

Chapter Twelve

Felix

Bram helped me find more mushrooms to make up for the ones I'd spilled, chatting away as he pulled himself through the grass with his one good arm and taking my mind off the stones I was sure must be hovering somewhere just beyond the line of mist. They might be asleep now the sun had come back out from behind the clouds, but I was pretty sure they still had one eye on me somewhere in the fog beyond the copse.

'So there's still no word of your pa, then?' Bram asked, jumping from one topic to another as fast as the weather changed. One minute he'd be talking about 'the wee fairy folk' whose houses we were stealing, the next he'd be asking how many soldiers were in a legion and whether I'd ever seen anyone get their head chopped off with a sword.

'No, we haven't heard anything since he left for the north at the start of spring. He should've been back from the mapping trip ages ago, I don't know why it's taking so long,' I sighed.

'Maybe he's walked right up to the edge of the world and fallen off?' Bram suggested. 'My grandma used to say that out past the hills, the sea just goes gushing down into a big empty hole at the world's end.'

'Thanks, Bram. Not helpful.' I stood up and stretched, trying to rub the tension from the back of my neck. I wasn't sure whether the ache was from picking mushrooms, keeping a lookout for signs of movement in the mist, or from lack of sleep worrying about what might have happened to my father.

'What's he like, your pa? Does he march around yelling orders at folk like them other metal men?'

'No, he doesn't need to shout to get the soldiers to obey him. He's strict, but he's fair, like a good school teacher, you know?'

'Uh-uh,' Bram shook his head. 'There's no skoo-well in our village. But we've plenty to learn about hunting, tilling the land and mixing medicines for the sick, and that's all taught by our Elders. The best of them are patient and don't shout when the bairns get things muddled up. I guess you mean your pa's like that, huh?'

'Sometimes. I mean he expects me to stick to the rules, but he always explains what the rules are for and why they should be followed. He doesn't just bark orders like a lot of the centurions. The men all respect him for that. So do I.' I bent down to rearrange the mushrooms in the basket again so that Bram wouldn't see the tears in my eyes. I had a lump in my throat the size of a crab apple that swelled up any time I thought about my father.

'Our Jinny wouldn't see eye to eye with him I'll bet,' Bram laughed, too busy making a sword out of two sticks tied up with grass to notice my distress. 'She's no mad keen on anyone who goes making rules in the first place. She and Pa are always at each other like two dogs over a bone. Ma says they're just too alike to get on – both of them want their own way and neither of them's willing to budge one hair's breadth.'

'So do you take after your mother then?' I asked to move the talk away from my father and onto safer ground.

'I reckon so. We both like to laugh more than growl, though Ma's got a habit of cooing over babies and pretty baubles and suchlike that I don't share. Pa used to say I had a thirst like him for the hunt and I'd make a fine warrior. He said he'd give me his best sword when I were bigger and teach me to fight with a shield. He's no said that for a while now. Guess that's the last I'll be hearing of that.' Bram looked in disgust at the stick sword he'd been making, then threw it across the copse. For the first time, I saw through the cracks in his smile to the hurt that was hidden just beneath.

'Bram, I'm so sorry. If there was anything I could do to make it up to you I'd–'

'I've got no more use for pity than you do, Roman boy, so stick it where the sun don't shine.' Bram frowned at me for a long moment, then the corners of his mouth turned back up. 'Sheesh, listen to me! I'm sounding more like Jinny than myself! Maybe there's a bit of her in me too.'

'No way, Bram. If you were like Jinny, you'd have bitten my head off by now just for breathing too much like a Roman,' I smiled.

'Is that what she did yesterday? Is that what you two were talking about?'

'Er... something like that,' I nodded. 'She saw me picking blackberries on Tintock Brae and she wasn't happy about it, that's all.'

'She saw you pinching our food for the metal men's dinner table and she didn't run you through with her wee knife on the spot?' Bram laughed. 'That's no like our Jinny. She must be going soft in her old age. Did she no give you an earful?'

'She made herself heard alright,' I shuddered, remembering the way she whistled and the way the stones seemed to move in the mist. I turned to look up at the slopes of Tintock Brae rising behind me. The sun was getting lower in the sky, the fog growing thicker as it curled up from the valley. It wouldn't be long before the stones were awake and walking again. And I was pretty sure they'd be coming for me.

'What about your ma?' Bram said suddenly, catching me off-guard. 'What were she like?'

'My mother?' The question surprised me so much I must've looked like a beached fish flapping my lips up and down gasping for air. No one had ever asked me about my mother before. Not once.

'Aye, your ma. She were a Damnonii just like the rest of us, though she were from a village way out west near New Kilpatrick, weren't she?'

'How in Jupiter's name did you know that? Who told you?' I didn't mean to sound defensive, but I'd been jealously guarding my mother's memory for so long against soldiers who said cruel things about her that it was out before I could stop it.

'My pa mentioned it once, is all. Said she were kicked out of the tribe for being with a Roman soldier instead of one of her own people.'

'And do you think it was wrong too?' I held my breath, waiting for Bram's answer like he was a senator in Rome passing judgement on my crime of being born half Roman and half tribe boy.

Bram shrugged like he couldn't care less either way. 'If that were wrong then you and me being friends is wrong too, and I don't see as how I got anything to be ashamed of in passing the day with you.'

That made me feel ten feet tall, and I couldn't help smiling like I'd just been handed a fortune in gold. 'Thanks, Bram.'

'What for? I'm only hanging around with you to annoy Jinny and get back at her for always calling my Tramper an ugly wee piglet with a saddle,' Bram grinned back. 'So... your ma then. You remember much about her?'

'Her kindness,' I nodded, 'and the way she teased my father when he got Damnonii words wrong. He'd pretend to be annoyed and pick her up like her was going to dump her in the river, and then he'd tickle her until she laughed so hard the soldiers would come and ask what all the noise was.' I didn't want to admit all the things I'd forgotten about her, like the sound of her voice and the exact colour of her hair. Instead I said, 'It's her stories I remember most. At night, in our tent when the camp was quiet and only the sentries on duty were awake, she used to tell me and my father all the legends of the Damnonii tribe.'

'Oh aye? And what ones did you like the best? I always liked the one about Bredon the hunter, but our Jinny likes the tales of the nixies in the marsh best.'

'I liked the one about the three trolls that live under a bridge at the Camsith Fells,' I said, smiling when a picture I didn't even know I'd remembered popped back into my head. 'My mother used to do all the voices for the three trolls. The high-pitched one for the littlest troll made me laugh, but the low one for the big troll made my hair stand on end.'

'Who's that trip-trip-trapping over MY bridge?' Bram

growled, then burst out laughing. 'Aye, I like that one too. I can just see me and Tramper trotting over the bridge and outfoxing them big smelly trolls with clever tricks, though I bet Jinny would just go right down there and give them one of her best temper fits and that would be the end of them. Handy thing, a fiery sister, when there's hungry trolls around.'

But not hungry stone giants, I thought, my smile fading. I looked back at the valley where the mist came swirling up and shivered. 'I didn't like the story about the stones in the sacred valley,' I said. 'That one kept me awake at night.'

'Me and all!' Bram agreed. 'There's no a soul in our tribe daft enough to go down the wrong side of Tintock Brae to the bottom of that valley and stand in the circle. Ailsa says you're fine as long as you sing and keep them asleep, but I'm no so sure. You and them metal men's just lucky you didn't go building your great big wall a couple of field lengths' further north, or you would've woken them up and had a deal of trouble getting them back to sleep again.'

'Is there a way to send them back to sleep again?' I asked eagerly. 'Once they've been woken up, I mean?'

'I don't know nothing about that. Why?' There was a slight edge of suspicion in Bram's voice, like he'd just noticed the way I kept staring into the mist and he'd put two and two together.

'No reason,' I said quickly. 'It's just my mother didn't tell me the rest of that legend, and I always wondered what the end of the story was.'

'Oh.' Bram's face relaxed. 'Far as I can guess, once you wake the stones up, then they'll go stomping about at night gobbling folk up till they're no hungry no more. They'll go back to sleep again once they've had their fill of man-flesh and they've chewed up the one who woke them in the first place. Least that's what my grandma used to say.'

'The one who woke them in the first place?' I gasped. 'Why him? Or her, I mean. It could just as easily be a "her",' I added.

'Grandma said it's the smell of the one who woke 'em that keeps them awake and they can't sleep till they've gobbled him up and got rid of the stench in their nostrils. Something like that anyhow. Most folk'll tell a different side of the story depending on what season it is and how much of the moon is showing,' Bram shrugged. 'Our Ailsa says most folk don't know their arse from their elbow when it comes to the truth of the stones in the circle.'

I didn't answer. I was too busy trying not to panic. *So it is me they want after all!* I thought, my heart thudding painfully when I remembered the way the stones had seemed to move when I stood in the circle. Jinny might've been the one who was whistling in the mist, but it was me they saw, and I was the one they'd blame for disturbing them. It was my scent they'd have in their nostrils when they went walking at night.

'It's time I got back,' I said, standing up and grabbing my basket. 'I've been out for ages and I'll get a beating if I don't get back with these mushrooms soon.'

'No worries, me and Tramper'll head down the Luggie and see if we can get any wee fishes for supper.'

'You ought to go straight back to your village, Bram. The sun'll be setting soon, and it's not safe to stay out late.'

'Don't fuss, you're no my ma, and there's ages of light

left,' Bram laughed. 'It's no even halfways to the gloaming.'

'But what about all those villagers disappearing?' I said, thinking of the meeting at the hallowed tree. 'What if there's a pack of wolves out hunting in these parts?'

Or what if it's something else? What if it was the stones that took those people away? I'd been so busy worrying the stones were coming after *me*, it hadn't occurred to me that they might not be too picky when they were hungry as long as they got a good meal. *Maybe that's what happened to those villagers last night,* I thought. *Maybe the stones couldn't get to me behind the wall, so they took those other people and ate them instead.*

'If it's wolves, then the hunters'll be halfway home with their skins by now,' Bram said, pulling himself over to the tree where he'd tied his pony up and undoing the long leather straps. 'And if it's the Maeatae from over the hills, they'll no be daft enough to go sneaking about on another tribe's turf two nights in a row, will they?'

I felt a bit awkward watching him struggle with the knots with only one good hand, not sure if I should offer to help him or let him get on with it. But he soon proved he'd figured out how to get back on his horse without anyone else interfering. He grabbed her reins, tugging them up and down till she gave in and bent her front knee to let him hop up into the saddle on his one whole leg. I felt like cheering, it was so good to see him back to his old self again.

'If I'd known you'd be back on a horse in a few months and riding about better than I can, I wouldn't have hidden away and felt so guilty about that accident,' I grinned, making a clumsy joke to hide my embarrassment.

'If I'd known you'd be a cheeky wee toad about my

misfortunes, I would've boxed your ears and kicked your backside when I'd two good hands and two legs attached,' Bram shot back. 'Don't push your luck, Roman boy.'

He was half smiling, but there was something lurking just behind that smile that made me ask, 'Are you sure you're alright, though, Bram? There's nothing I can do for you? Nothing I can bring from the fort for you, you know, like I used to?'

'There is one thing you can do for me,' Bram nodded, 'though I can't rightly say you'll like it much.'

'What is it? I'll do anything you need.' I knew it wasn't really my fault that Bram fell into the spike pits that day, but if I could just pay some sort of fine or penalty then it might help me get over the last of the lingering guilt. I thought he might ask me to do something difficult, but it turned out to be something I'd already sworn to myself I'd do anyway.

'I need you to promise me you'll no betray someone else's secret again,' Bram said seriously. 'Bad things happen when you tell folk things they're no supposed to know. People get hurt, even when you don't mean them to, and you think you're doing the right thing. Promise me you'll never do it again.'

'I've learned my lesson, Bram.' I held out my hand, and shook his solemnly. 'I promise I won't betray another secret. Not ever.'

'That's settled then,' Bram grinned, giving Tramper a kick and setting her jogging back up towards the fields. 'See you around, Roman boy. Watch out for the wolves and the angry fairy folk who'll want to know what you've done with their pretty wee houses!'

'See you later, Bram.'

I watched till he disappeared over the hill, then I crossed the copse and headed back across the wide stretch of grass that sloped up to the wall. I didn't turn back to see if there was anything watching me from the mist this time. I was certain now that there was.

Brutus had a job waiting for me back at camp, and it turned out to be the worst job I'd ever had to do in my whole life. It made me ashamed to be a Roman, and scared that the Damnonii would think I was just as bad as the soldiers if they found out. I had to swear to Brutus I wouldn't say a word of it to anyone outside the fort, but in the end, I couldn't keep the secret to myself.

But even though I broke my promise to Bram, I still couldn't stop the terrible things that happened next.

Chapter Thirteen

Jinny

That night the stones went walking again. I were sure they did. I saw them.

And no just that, I heard them and all. They were whistling to me through the dark, I could swear it.

After I'd helped Ma with the turnip stew and chased the chickens back into the big barn down by the milking shed for the night, I went for a last look out over the fence afore I turned in. The wind were right noisy, lifting the thatch clean off the village huts in tufts and rattling the gates like they weren't no more than a collection of sticks tied up with grass. A couple of big lads were at the lookout posts, clutching their tartans tight in the teeth of the biting wind and grumbling about the cold, but the Elders weren't taking any chances after the vanishings and had doubled the night watch on the front and back gates.

I slipped round to a dark patch of fence behind the blacksmith's forge, rolling a barrel over quiet as I could and climbing up to look out into the night. The wind whipped the clouds across the moon fast as an owl in flight, the fields beyond the village lit up ghostly pale one moment and cloaked in shadow the next. I fixed my eyes on the outline of Tintock Brae against the troubled sky, looking for signs of movement from the path of the sacred valley. After what Ailsa said about whistling being the thing that wakes the stones and sends them walking home, it were likely to be me and my village they'd be heading for to fill their bellies.

Curse that nasty wee Roman boy and the troubles he's brought down on us! I scowled to myself, trying to burn off the jitters with red hot anger. It used to work whenever I felt guilty about my part in the accident. If ever I had doubts that I should've kept a cooler head that day and just let them metal men have the rabbits and be done with it, I thought about the Roman boy and how it were all his fault. The thought of how he betrayed my wee brother's secret and brought the soldiers to our copse usually set my blood boiling with outrage. But no this time. This time it were all on me. I were the one who took his basket of brambles and led him down through the mist into the sacred circle. I were the one who tried to knock his head off and woke the stones with my whistling and my badly-slung rock. Now the stones were walking the night and carrying off the tribesfolk, and I had no one to blame but myself.

The fear of seeing them coming for me through the dark were stronger than any of the misplaced anger I'd felt afore. My knuckles were white with the dread of it as I clutched the top of the fence posts and prayed to the four winds to deliver me and my village from the evil I'd done. There weren't no answer, save for the clouds speeding faster and the shadows lengthening over the frost-capped fields.

They're no coming this way, I sighed at last, rubbing my tired eyes and blowing on my numb fingers to feel them tingle with life again.

I were just about to climb down and get back to my warm bedroll when I heard it. Low and soft on the wind it came, a tune of war and loss and sadness that sent shivers down my spine with its haunting notes. I'd know the song in my sleep, so deep it were etched in my memory. But this weren't no grandma's lullaby as she rocked a bairn on her knee, nor a shepherd singing to his sheep as he brought the flock home at sundown. This were the distant breath of danger in the mist, sending its warning signal ahead on the wind.

The stones were whistling to me in the dark.

They were coming after all.

In the next flash of moonlight through the racing clouds, I saw one of them clear as day, standing at the edge of the kale field and waiting for the next patch of darkness to cross. They didn't come at you when you were looking straight at them, oh no. They snuck up on you in the mist and the shadows, all quiet and thief-like. It were huge, that stone giant, all hunched and misshapen with a hundred-score seasons of standing in the driving rain and snow. I thought I saw a face in the grey rock, two hollow eyes above a gaping black mouth. But then the moon disappeared behind the clouds once more, almost as though the night were holding its breath.

When the moon dared to peek back out again, there were two of them.

A second stone had crept out of the dark to stand gazing at me from the far side of the field. It were that first stone that made me clamp my hand to my mouth to stop me from screaming out loud, though. It were no longer at the far side of the kale row. Now it were halfway across the field, so close I could see the big lump of rock missing from its head, like someone had gouged out one of its eyes. It were the stone giant I'd torn a chunk out of with my sling.

I toppled backwards off the barrel in fright, landing in

a heap in the grass with my breath all knocked out of me. Afore I could let the fear freeze me to the spot, I jumped up again, racing to the warning bell by the village gate. I untied it, never minding the shouts from the lads on guard to leave the thing well alone, and began swinging the big bell rope with all my might. It didn't take long afore the clanging woke the whole village.

'What in the name of the moon spirit is going on out here?' Gregor demanded when he came racing up and saw it were me sending up the racket and no the gate guards.

I were too full of dread at what I'd seen to be afeared of the bother I'd be in with the Council of Elders for bashing the warning bell without permission, so I shouted to anyone who'd listen, 'It's the sacred stones! The giants are up and about and heading straight this way! I saw them in the dark! I heard them calling!'

A whole crowd of sleepy faces looked back at me like I were raving mad.

'The lass is havering!' one of the guards said. 'Me and Orin have been watching the fields since sundown, and we've no seen so much as a rabbit heading this way.'

'It's true, I swear!' I yelled, grabbing my pa's arm and pulling him to the fence. 'See for yourself! The stones are almost upon us!'

Pa gave me the same look he usually threw my way when I told him I'd weeded the fields when I'd plainly done no more than pick the daisies and make a whole pile of pretty bracelets. But he stepped up to the guard post and peered out into the night anyway, his brow creased with worry. I weren't sure if he were more afraid that I were telling the truth about the stones, or that I'd made the story up to get attention and shamed him in front of the crowd.

When he finally stepped down and came back to us, I knew from his face that he weren't never going to believe a word I said ever again.

'There's nothing out there, Jinny,' he frowned. 'It's just shadows in the moonlight. What did you think you were doing waking the whole village to tell us your silly stories? What in the name of the four winds has got into you these days?'

'But it's true!' I wailed, seeing the fear in the villagers' eyes turn to anger at my mischief. 'I saw them plain as day!' I jumped up on the guard post, elbowing aside the big lad who stood there and gazing out across the fields where I'd seen the stones coming at me through the dark. There were nothing there now save the scraps of bushes and stunted trees swaying in the wind. The fields were empty.

'But I know I saw...' I trailed off, the dread of the anger I saw in Gregor's eyes replacing my former fright. 'I'm no making up stories!' I insisted. 'The stones are awake and walking, I know it! What d'you think took Connor and the rest of the folk the other night, huh? The hunters never found them wolves, nor so much as a hair on a Maeatae bandit's head! If it weren't the stones, then where did them four folk vanish to? Tell me that!'

The villagers all set to muttering and climbing up the fence to look out over the fields themselves. They might not believe me, but ever since the disappearances, they'd been jumpy as a band of fleas on a dung heap. It didn't take long for the muttering to turn to grumbling about me being a daft wee slip of a lass who were so desperate for notice, she'd turned the whole village out of their beds with her clamouring.

'Jinny, your mischief making has got to stop,' Gregor growled at me so fierce I thought he were going to bite my head off and spit it halfway to Tintock Brae. 'You've scared folk half to death tonight with your silly stories, and all for the sake of a bit of attention. I'm sure the rest of the Elders agree with me that the best way to put an end to your mischief is to keep you too busy to make up any more of your nonsense.'

The four other Elders nodded, looking at me sternly. Ailsa's face were pale, like she were sick with worry and losing sleep over her Connor. That made me feel even worse than the thought of all the extra chores I'd be doing from now till forever to make up for ringing the bell.

'Donall, get her home and make sure she stays out of mischief for once,' Gregor told my pa. 'She needs a firmer hand to keep her in check, and a pile of work to keep her busy from now on.'

Pa looked ready to sink into the ground with shame at the rebuke. He took my arm none too gently and led me through the crowd, pretending no to hear the rude remarks that were flung after us. But the way his jaw clenched, I knew he were feeling the sting of every one.

'Why can you no just do what you're told, Jinny?' he said without looking at me as we headed for our hut. 'Why can you no just be a good lass like the rest of them? You've near broke your ma's heart with fretting over you, and made me too ashamed to hold my head up with the other men of the village.'

I couldn't answer. I had a lump in my throat so big, it were choking all the air out of me. 'Sorry, Pa,' I tried to

121

say, but it came out as a wee sob that sounded so much like I were pitying myself, my pa just shook his head and pushed me into the hut, sending me to bed without a kind word to see me off. Ma went hurrying out to ask him what the fuss were about, and she stood outside with Pa for half an age, whispering with him so low I couldn't catch their words even though I near strained my ears off with trying.

'Jinny, what's amiss? What were the bell ringing for?'

Bram sat up in his bedroll in the corner of our wee hut, his eyes bright in the moonlight that were peeking through the wooden slats of the walls.

'It were a false alarm, Bram, go back to sleep,' I muttered, curling up in my own bedroll and turning my face away.

'Aw, c'mon Jin!' Bram shook me. 'I've been sitting here near peeing myself with the need to know what's been going on. Pa were up and away afore I could get him to give me a piggyback, and Ma wouldn't let me out of the hut for fear I'd run into danger. I'm sick of being kept out of things like a helpless wee bairn. Don't treat me like that, Jin, no you.'

I sat back up, wiping away the tears that had rolled down my cheeks despite me biting my lip hard to keep them in.

'It were my fault, Bram,' I sighed, 'as usual. I went and rung the warning bell and now everyone thinks I'm the wickedest imp that ever walked the earth. Why can I no do anything right?'

'But what did you go making such a clamour for?' Bram asked afore I could melt in a sorry wee puddle of self-pity. 'Did you see something out in the dark?'

'I thought I saw the sacred stones out walking. I thought they were heading our way across the fields to steal the village folk away, but it turns out it were just shadows in the moonlight.' I was sure of what I'd seen, but I'd no get anyone else to believe me, no now.

'What made you think the stones went walking? Did you wake them up, Jin? Ach, our Jinny-o-the-autumn, say you never did anything so wicked!'

I hesitated. I were ready to burst with the need to share my secret with Bram. But seeing the anger of the villagers at my mischief, the sadness in Ma's eyes at my failings, and the disappointment and shame I'd heaped upon Pa, I couldn't stand to have my wee brother look at me like the rest of them did. And so I lied to the one person I loved most in the whole wide world.

'Of course not, Bram! Where'd you get such a mad idea?'

'I'm no accusing you of nothing, Jinny!' he said quickly, his scarred wee face all trusting and innocent. 'It's just Felix were asking the other day about sending the stones back to sleep, and it got me to wondering–'

'That Roman boy were asking about the stones?' I pounced on this as an excuse faster than a hungry dog seizing a scrap of rotten meat. 'Then he's the reason they're walking abroad, I'd stake my life on it! The other day on Tintock Brae, he went running off into the mist and I bet he went and woke the stones down in the sacred valley.'

'Felix wouldn't do nothing that stupid, Jin! He knows the story as well as we do.'

'Does he, now?' I scowled, annoyed at the thought of that smug wee Roman claiming our legends as his own, just like them arrogant metal men claimed our land and our wild game for their cooking pot. 'He's clever, that one. He's worked out we'll no give up our berries and game without a fight, so he's woken the stones to chase us off our land!'

'That don't sound like something Felix would do.' Bram looked upset at the very thought.

'Does it no?' I pressed on, eager to shift all my guilt and blame onto someone else. 'I'll bet you would've said sharing your secret with the metal men weren't something he'd have done neither. And if he felt so bad at his part in your accident, how come he's no been to see you once since then, hmm?' A wee voice at the back of my head reminded me of the time – a new moon or so after the accident – when I'd caught the Roman boy coming across the fields to check on Bram and I'd sent him packing with a flea in his ear and a big bruise on his shin. But I thought better of sharing that story.

Bram were looking confused, like he were trying to puzzle out something that didn't make a lick of sense. 'But Felix is my friend,' he said sadly. 'I mean, I think he is.'

'You can't trust a Roman, Bram, no even one who speaks our language. It's best to trust no one at all. That way, folks won't take advantage of your good nature.'

'But I can trust you, though, Jinny, can't I?' Bram's eyes were wide with hope, and I felt my guts twist with shame in the darkness.

''Course you can, Bram. I'd no tell you stories that weren't true.'

'And you saw the stones out walking, for real? You think it's them that took Connor and the other folk?' He grabbed my hand in the dark and held on tight with worry.

'Don't you go fretting about that. I'll get them sent back to sleep soon enough, and the place'll be as safe as it ever was. Get some sleep, Bram, we've got a deal of work coming up these next few days to make ready for the autumn festival.'

Bram huddled back up in his bedroll, pulling the blankets over his head to keep out the chill. He kept hold of my hand the whole time it took him to fall asleep, his fingers only letting go when he were dreaming once more. But I couldn't sleep a wink that night. No after Ma and Pa came back in and went to sleep themselves. No even when the whole village were silent and the wind died down in the early light of morning. The whole long, lonely time till the cocks started their dawn crowing, I were heartsick and guilt-ridden as a cutthroat killer on the way to the chopping block.

I weren't worried about the extra chores I'd been set by the Elders, nor even the angry looks of the other villagers. I were well used to all that by now. No, it were lying to Bram that were eating me up from the inside out. If I didn't get them stones sent back to sleep, they'd come walking again for sure, and I'd have more vanishings on my conscience than I could take in one lifetime. If Bram ever found out what I'd done and looked at me with sadness or disappointment like Ma or Pa did, it'd break my heart clean in two. I had to find a way to soothe the stones and set them dreaming once more, and I had to find it fast.

In five sundowns' time, it would be Samhain, the night when the veil between our world and the world of the uncanny creatures of the dark would be stretched so thin they could just drift across with no more effort than a hand brushing away a cobweb. If ever there were a night when the stones would have the strength to walk right up to our village and cross our gate all warded with witching charms and magic to keep the uncanny things of the night out, it would be Samhain.

I didn't have much time.

Chapter Fourteen

Felix

There were only four more nights until the Damnonii's Samhain festival. That was how the tribespeople marked time – not by days and weeks and months, but by moons and seasons, sun-rises and feast days. Romans marked time far more precisely, but I wished with all my heart we didn't. I'd been carrying my secret around for just two days, but already it felt like a lifetime. Every hour that I kept it to myself was torture. I wanted to go running to the Damnonii villages to tell them what I knew, but I couldn't. I wasn't sure whether it was my promise to Bram not to share another secret that kept me silent, or whether it was my fear of what Brutus would do if I opened my mouth. Either way, I felt dirty, stained by my crimes even though I'd been given no choice about the part I had to play in them.

As my mind wandered away from kitchen work, the knife slipped in my hand and a row of blood beads welled up on my thumb. I threw down the mussel I'd been prising open and sucked it, wishing it was as easy to wash away my guilt.

'Careful with that, boy!' the head cook warned. 'We don't want you poisoning our Legate's *cena* with your tribe blood. Finish shelling those crayfish, then go and tell the new slaves to start on the washing up.'

Brutus had solved the Senior Tribune's slave problem just like he'd promised. There were four brand new slaves housed in the prison block till they could be trusted not to try to escape, freeing the rest of the officers' slaves up from kitchen chores to serve at the Tribunes' table. I should've been happy at the news I no longer had to fetch and carry for the Senior Tribune's dinner parties. I was still being used as an errand boy, but at least I had time now for school. All I had to do on top of my evening kitchen work was translate the orders of the kitchen staff for the new slaves and show them what to do.

They didn't speak a word of Latin. Of course they didn't. They were Damnonii.

I finished shelling and set down my knife, heading over to the table where two of the new slaves were hunched over chopping fruit for the Legate's dessert. He'd come back to our fort for the night to issue fresh orders, requisition supplies and transfer several more of the second Augustan's cohorts to the New Kilpatrick fort. Apparently, things were really hotting up over there with the locals, and he needed reinforcements. It made me shiver to think what would happen to Bram's village if the rebellion spread, or the tribespeople found out the Romans at Caerpen Taloch had taken four of their people prisoner. That was part of the peace treaty negotiated sixteen years ago when the wall was built. No slave captures in return for an uneasy peace. From where I stood, all-out war was starting to look more and more likely.

'The cook says you've to wash the cooking pots and the bowls coming back from the dining room,' I told the man and woman slicing apples and preserved pears at the table. The woman snorted and didn't look up, but the man turned to stare at me like he wanted to peel my face off with the paring knife he was holding.

'Tell the cook to shove the dishes up his arse,' he growled. 'We're no doing any more work till we get a decent meal ourselves.'

Well, that was an improvement from yesterday. Last night they used carving knife swords and wooden platter shields to stage a slaves' revolt in the garrison cookhouse, and the day before that when they'd first been captured, they had to be chained up in the prison block to stop them trying to escape. I'd hated having to translate orders for Brutus that day. He told them that if they ran away, the Roman legion would descend on their villages in full force and raze them to the ground. Then yesterday, I had to tell them if they ever tried to fight back again, their villages would be burned, and their hands would be chopped off for daring to strike a Roman. Today it was worse: if they didn't do exactly as they were told, their villages would be burned, their hands chopped off, and any surviving family members sold to the Circus in Rome. That finally got them following orders, but their obedience didn't make me feel any better about my own orders.

'Look, I don't like this any more than you do,' I sighed. 'But I have to do as I'm told too, and I've been told to get you to do the washing up. I'm sorry about all this, I really am, but what can I do?'

The slave gave me a hard stare that was full of contempt. I'd seen him before in Bram's village the few times I'd been there before the accident, I was sure of it. I hadn't asked any of the slaves their names yet. I was afraid that if I learned anything about them, I'd end up feeling so bad I'd either explode, or do something stupid like help them escape. Either way, it would end badly for me. The soldiers had given them numbers till they were docile enough to be given Latin names, but I was pretty sure I'd heard the woman call this man glaring at me 'Connor'.

'What can *you* do?' Connor snorted in disgust. 'You can find us a way out of here, that's what. And if that's too much bother, then the least you can do is go to Waterside and tell my village chief that we've been captured. Gregor will find a way to make the Romans release us.'

'I can't do that!' I protested. 'If I help you, I'll get thrown out of the fort! And what if your people decide to get revenge and start a war with the Romans? I don't want to be responsible for people dying!'

'If you can't take responsibility for doing the right thing, then what use are you to anyone?' the woman snapped, her knife chopping dangerously close to my fingers. I snatched them back, feeling guilty and helpless all at the same time.

'It might just be for a short time,' I said, knowing it was a lie as soon as the words left my mouth. 'The legion might let you go when–'

'By Jupiter, that's an awful lot of words just to get them to do the washing up!' one of the soldiers guarding the slaves snapped at me. 'If they're giving any trouble, then a taste of my sword will be the antidote to their laziness.' He took a step towards the two slaves, half drawing his sword from his sheath in warning. Connor and the woman didn't need a translation for that. They quickly got to work with the water buckets and piles of dirty dishes stacked up on the floor. The two other slaves stoking the fire and stirring the pots kept their heads down, but their silence was every bit as much an accusation as the woman's words.

When I finally got out of the hot kitchen and into the fresh night air, my head was pounding and my heart was so heavy I could almost feel it clunking around in my boots. Nothing had gone right at the fort since my father left. Everything was a mess, and I was tangled up in it like a helpless kitten in a ball of string. If only my father had been here, then Bram would never have had his accident, Brutus would never have been promoted to acting Camp Prefect, and there wouldn't be four Damnonii slaves in the kitchens threatening our fragile peace treaty with the local tribe. If only I knew what to do about it all. But I was so lost and confused without my father here to guide me that all I could do was blindly follow the orders the soldiers gave me, and hope that would be enough to prove I still deserved my place in the fort.

I climbed up onto the wall walkway, resting my head against the palisade and looking out into the night. I was too tired to be afraid of the stone giants. Now that I knew it was the soldiers and not the stones that had made those four villagers disappear, I was starting to wonder if I hadn't just imagined what I saw in the sacred circle. It was probably just one of Jinny's tricks to make sure I didn't sleep at night. She shouldn't have bothered – I hadn't had a good night's sleep since my father left.

'Marcus Lucius Aquila Felix!' a voice said right behind me, and a hand clapped down on my shoulder, making me jump. I spun round, half expecting a beating for laziness or at the very least, another set of chores to keep me up till midnight. But when I saw who it was, I couldn't help grinning so hard my face hurt.

'Legate Octavius Clarus! It's so good to see you again,

sir.'

'Likewise, my boy, likewise,' the legion commander smiled down at me. His grey hair was shot with white and his breastplate didn't sit as well as it once did over his tunic, but he still looked fit enough to face an army of Damnonii warriors and come out with his pride intact.

'How have you been getting on, Felix, hmm? Still the eager scholar I'll bet, eh? Keep at the books, my boy, your father didn't neglect his reading, and he was a better soldier for it.'

'Has there been any word from him and his cohort? Anything at all?' I asked hopefully. I already knew what the answer would be, but I was still disappointed by the Legate's loud sigh.

'I'm afraid we have to assume the worst in his case. It's a bad business, but without support from Rome, we won't be sending any more expeditions north. The way things are going, we won't be here much longer either, but best not talk politics and bore you, eh, my boy?'

The Legate smiled and clapped me on the shoulder again, but I could see the worry lines etched into his forehead. It took me a moment to work out that one of the many things he was worried about was me.

'You're happy at the fort, aren't you, Felix? You'll want to follow in your father's footsteps I'll bet, eh?'

'Of course, sir. As soon as I'm old enough I want to be a soldier and join the army.'

'Good, good! Glad to hear that. I just thought that perhaps with your father gone and your mother being, ahem, you know, one of the northerners, you might feel more comfortable elsewhere if the legion were to move on.'

'Move on? Where sir? Are there orders to–'

'No, nothing like that! Nothing to concern you anyway, my boy. But you're sure it's the Roman way for you in the future?'

The Legate had never questioned my desire to join the army before. With my father gone and the other soldiers treating me little better than the Damnonii, I was worried my place here as a Roman was rapidly slipping through my grasp.

'Sir, has the Senior Centurion been saying anything about me? I know he wants the full promotion to my father's post, but I haven't been–'

'Relax, my boy, relax. No one's been telling tales. None that I want to hear anyway. But you have to understand, the peace we have here with the tribespeople, it's a fragile thing, you know. And if anything were to threaten that peace, even the most offhand gossip that reached the villages, we could have a whole new war on our hands, you see?'

'Ah.' I finally understood what he was asking. He wanted to know if I was going to stay loyal to the legion or go blabbing to the Damnonii about the prisoners that Brutus had installed in the officers' kitchen. 'I know there's a lot at stake, sir. I'm not one to go flapping my tongue at anyone who'll listen.'

Bram might not entirely agree with that, but now I'm stuck with this secret whether I like it or not, I thought.

'That's good to hear, my boy. Well done.' The Legate looked relieved. 'I'm not happy about the slave situation either, and the orders certainly didn't come from me. But now that they're here, we have to make the best of things. They really aren't any different from any of the other slaves we have, you know. Perfectly good Roman policy, slave holding, keeps everything running smoothly, eh?'

'Yes, sir. I understand that, sir.' I nodded, even though it hurt to lie to this man who'd always been kind to me. The truth was, they weren't the same as the other slaves at all. Most of the rest had been born slaves or sold so young they couldn't remember a different life. Some of them even seemed to like the security of food and shelter every day in exchange for the work they did. I'd never really thought much about how the slaves felt about their position before, but now, seeing the anger and desperation in the eyes of the four Damnonii captives, I realised just how wrong it was to deprive people of their freedom. And that made me feel like the worst traitor to Rome in the whole world.

'Well, my boy, you ought to be getting along to bed, don't you think? School tomorrow, books to read, that sort of thing, eh?'

'Yes, sir. Goodnight, sir.'

As I climbed back down the turf slope, I saw why I was being dismissed. Brutus and the Senior Tribune were heading along the top of the wall towards the Legate, looking like a couple of guilty children who'd been caught with their hands in the preserved fruit jar. The Legate clearly hadn't been too impressed when he heard his *cena* had been prepared by a group of Damnonii captives.

I pretended to head for the tent camp, but then doubled back behind the administration block, ducking under a high wooden guard tower to listen in on the officers' conversation. I knew it was wrong, but I had to find out if the Damnonii slaves were going to get sent home before I exploded with guilt for not telling the other villagers what had happened to them.

At first they talked in voices too low for me to hear, making sure the soldiers on sentry duty couldn't catch what they were saying. But when the guard changed on the hour, they moved closer to the spot where I was hiding, and I heard the rest of their conversation.

'By Jupiter, I thought you had more sense than this, Aurelius Taurus!' the Legate snapped at the second-in-command. 'I'm gone a few days and you have our peace treaty dangling from a rope with its backside hanging out for all to see.'

'We were badly understaffed,' Taurus said smoothly, clearly used to having to defend his decisions to his commanding officer. 'I had to take steps to keep the kitchens running after you requisitioned so many of our slaves for the New Kilpatrick fort, or discipline here would've broken down entirely.'

'I fail to see what your dinner parties for every nobleman between here and Hadrian's Wall have to do with fort discipline!' the Legate shot back. There was an uncomfortable silence for a long moment, then Brutus cleared his throat.

'Sir, if I may? There's no danger of the slaves here being discovered. The half-blood boy has already informed us that the local villagers think the four captives were either eaten by wolves or carried off by the savage tribe from beyond the northern hills, so there really is no need to worry about repercussions.'

'Glad to hear it! But that still doesn't excuse your actions. The Senate has made it very clear there's to be no more action here on the Empire's northern frontier. They've lost their appetite for further expansion, and we're expecting orders to withdraw south any week now. '

'*What?*' Taurus snorted. 'That's ridiculous! The glory of Rome is at stake here! If we withdraw then those savages will think they've conquered our army! Our honour will be trampled to dust!'

'Hardly, Taurus. Don't exaggerate,' the Legate sighed. 'I doubt the Damnonii will notice one way or the other whether we're here or not. Whatever your personal feelings, this northern outpost has proven very costly, and the Senate is tired of funding a campaign that has sent very little back to Rome in return. We're on standby to withdraw, and until those orders arrive, DO NOT do anything which might antagonise the tribespeople further, do you understand me? I'm doing my best to resolve the situation in New Kilpatrick as quickly and peacefully as I can, so I expect there to be no more slaves turning up in my kitchens until I return. Those are my orders. Ensure they're carried out.'

'Yes, sir.'

'Of course, sir.'

Taurus and Brutus sounded like they were chewing on nettles.

I heard the Legate's footsteps fading away, and I stood still for a long moment, waiting to hear if the coast was clear for me to sneak back to the tents. Before I could move, the other two officers started talking in low voices again.

'What do you think of that then, Brutus?' the Senior Tribune said in disgust. 'After all our hard work here, we're to be sent back to Hadrian's Wall with our tails between our legs, as though this venture has been an embarrassing failure instead of a glorious success!'

'It's hard to believe, sir. I can only think the Senate must be unaware of how important this wall is to the security of the Empire.'

Important? Huh! I had to bite my tongue to keep from laughing at that. All that the Roman army had managed to do here was have a disastrous fight with the locals, take over their land then build a big turf wall and sit behind it for over fifteen years hoping the tribespeople would see how much better it would be for them to submit to the might of Rome and join the Empire. The army just didn't have the troops or the provisions to wage a long war or push any further north. From what I'd seen, the Damnonii were less than impressed with the Roman's efforts to 'civilise' them.

Then Taurus said something that made me instantly swallow my smile.

'The only way to convince the Senate how important this wall is for the protection of the Empire, is to prove just how big a threat those savages are to the Roman army.'

'That sounds very sensible, sir.' There was a nasty edge of glee in Brutus's voice now.

'But we can't antagonise the locals by taking more slaves, of course. We don't want to go against our Legate's orders, do we?'

'Of course not, sir. But I think I know the very thing that would have every single barbarian in the wilderness banging on our gate begging for a fight.'

'Of course you do, Brutus. That's why you're so useful to me,' Taurus laughed. 'Now, what's your plan?'

As I stood there listening to the voices whispering in the darkness, I felt the cold hand of dread claw its way up my spine and wrap its fingers round my heart. If Brutus and Taurus put their plan into action, there would be war with the Damnonii for sure, and no one would be able to stop it.

No one except me.

Chapter Fifteen

Jinny

It were three sundowns to go till Samhain, and we weren't none of us in much of a celebrating mood no more.

This were usually my favourite time of year, what with the leaves on the trees all a flame of red and orange, the cider fresh pressed in the barrels and the promise of mutton pie to come and all. No this year. This year the vanishings had taken the shine right out of the golden sunlight, and my fear of the walking stones had me trembling like a newborn lamb every time the wind whistled over the fields. And that were afore I even thought on the trouble I were in for raising a false alarm with the warning bell last night.

Everyone in the village had a job to do to prepare for the feast, and they all made sure they gave me the most reeking stink-eye they could manage while they went about it. The four new-made women muttered about me under their breath as they churned the butter by the milking shed, the older women making a point of ignoring me as they worked on turning out the small wheels of cheese.

'No stooping to give me the attention I were bidding for' were how Ailsa put it.

The menfolk who weren't up on the sheiling with the sheep and cattle were working on putting up the long trestle tables and benches for the feast, while the hunters had gone out early stalking deer and smaller game for the pot. They paid me no mind neither, but the looks of pity they threw my pa as he whittled the wood with his long knife were enough to tell me what they thought of him having such a daughter as me.

Even the wee bairns kept their distance as they worked, getting the old collection baskets into shape and repairing the holes with fresh reeds and wicker. Them baskets were special, that's why they were kept and reused for mistletoe gathering every year. At midnight tonight, we'd all traipse out to the hallowed tree and watch the Elders cut big clumps of mistletoe down to hang around our village fence to ward off the evil spirits walking abroad on Samhain. All the villages in tramping distance of the tree came for their mistletoe at the same time, so it were an important event that no one liked to miss out on. I'd just have to wait and see if I'd be allowed to go along this year, what with all the trouble I were in with the Council.

This morning I were given the worst job of the lot. I were made to clean out all the cups and pitchers and pots and tankards for serving the cider and honey mead at the festival. The special jugs and all were only used a couple of times a year and stored in the Council hut along with the carved knives and ritual herbs for magic ceremonies, so they were right fusty and covered with grime from sitting for so long. I had to lug buckets back and forth to the stream five times afore I had enough water to scrub them all out, and even then, there were two cups and a big pitcher I just couldn't get the mould out of.

'Ach, Bram, I give up! I'm too puggled to go stomping down to the Luggie again just for the sake of these couple of things. You think anyone'll notice if the table's two cups and a jug short at Samhain?' I asked hopefully.

'It's a fair bet that Ailsa will,' my wee brother said,

stopping by on his way to bring our pa another saw for the table legs. 'That one good eye of hers sees more 'n the eyes of the whole village put together.'

'Aye, you're probably right,' I sighed, picking up one of the buckets again. 'Sheesh, though! My feet are worn flat with tramping back and forth and my hands are that sore from scrubbing, I'll be worn to a bony wee skeleton by the time Samhain comes round.'

'I could give you a ride,' Bram suggested. 'Tramper'll no mind carrying us both down to the Luggie, will you, girl?' He patted his horse's neck, and she turned to take a bite out of his sleeve in reply.

'You're supposed to be fetching tools for the bench-building, and Pa'll think we're up to something if we go riding out of sight downstream.'

'Ach, Jin, I'm going clear out of my mind with the boredom of this bairn's work!' Bram sighed. 'There's wee ones just five summers' old that can fetch the bits of wood and tools for the builders, it's no like they're using any planks bigger than a bairn's leg for the work. I need to get out of here for a stretch or I'll burst with the dullness of it!'

I bit my lip, feeling the big cooking pot of anger, pity and guilt bubbling up inside me at the thought of my wee brother stuck doing chores fit only for the tiniest bairns of the village. It were so unfair I wanted to scream. Last year, Bram had gone out with the hunters, bagging two rabbits with his bow and arrow and helping fell the biggest stag our village had ever seen. Pa were so proud of him, I thought his chest were going to explode it were that puffed up. But this year, it were all different. A hunter needs two strong arms for the bow, but Bram needed his one good arm for holding Tramper's reins. I could see he were worried that hunting work were going to be forever out of his reach now.

Connor, the head herder, had been on at Ma and Pa to let him train Bram up for work on the sheilings afore he vanished, but Ma weren't mad keen on letting Bram out of her sight for so long every day, no when the memory of the accident were still so fresh in her mind. So now he were stuck in the village, doing the work of wee bairns like he were being punished alongside his wicked big sister. But I'd no earned my share of the punishment any more than Bram had; I'd just tried to keep the village safe from the stones last night. I could spit I were so mad at the unfairness of it.

I'd spent the whole scrubbing time this morning trying to puzzle out a way of keeping them stones from going walking again. The mistletoe gathering ceremony set for tonight were what cracked it in the end. Folks leaving the safety of the village while the moon were up were a big problem. If the stones went stomping about looking for meat tonight, and all the villagers were up at the hallowed tree near the valley gathering mistletoe, then that would be the most dangerous place in the whole wide world. With such easy pickings standing right on the stone giants' doorstep, someone were bound to get eaten right in front of us, and I couldn't take the guilt of anyone else being hurt on account of my mistakes.

But what were we gathering that mistletoe for in the first place? To hang around our village fence to keep the spirits of Samhain at bay! See? I just had to gather a bunch of mistletoe afore tonight and spread it round the stone circle, and that would keep the giants from breaking out of the valley and munching any more of the villagers. I could kick myself for no thinking of it afore now. But if I snuck out of the village and went marching off to the hallowed tree just now, it'd take five times as long as a trip down to the Luggie to fetch a bucket of water. I were already being watched by everyone in the village over the age of ten summers for signs of shirking. I couldn't risk going to the tree on foot, no even if I ran. But with Tramper, I could do it in half the time.

'Bram, it's more than a ride to the Luggie I need just now. I have to get to the hallowed tree and back afore anyone misses me and tells the Council I'm shirking my chores again.'

'But we're going to the tree tonight, Jin, can you no wait till then?' Bram asked.

'Tonight'll be too late!'

'For what?'

'Remember I told you the other night the stone giants were awake and walking the fields? Well, I need to put them to sleep afore folk all leave the safety of their villages and meet up at the tree tonight. If I can gather some mistletoe and spread it round the circle, it'll keep all the evil things inside from getting out. And then everyone will be safe, see?'

Bram grinned and nodded enthusiastically. He didn't mind breaking the rules as long as it were for a good cause. 'Best jump up quick then afore Tramper decides she's had enough work for the day and gets stubborn.'

I glanced over to the milking shed where Ma were hard at work with the cheese cloths. Her head were down and she were talking in whispers with Ailsa, no doubt about me and my waywardness, so she weren't going to miss us for the short time it would take to get to the hallowed tree on horseback.

'Right, Bram, let's go. But we'll need to get back fast as we can, mind – we'd best no look like we're shirking or you'll get a share of the trouble I'm in.'

I clambered up onto Tramper's back with my leather pouch and knife ready for gathering a pile of mistletoe. The wee pony grumbled and snorted, pawing and kicking till she realised I weren't going to get off. Then she plodded slowly out the gates with her hoofs scraping the ground so I'd know how much bother I were causing her. It were only a short trip across the fields to the meadow, but it felt like I were free to breathe for the first time once I'd got away from the accusing eyes of the villagers who all blamed me for their lack of sleep the other night.

Bram gave Tramper a kick and she settled into a grumpy trot, bouncing us up and down as much as she could to get us to give up and turn back. But Bram were well used to her moodiness, and I were too eager to sort out the bother I'd caused with the sacred stones to pay her any mind. By the time we got to the hallowed tree, though, my backside were as sore as my hands and feet, and I were starting to wish I'd just run all the way over by myself instead.

'Right, keep a lookout for me, Bram,' I said, jumping down and pulling out my knife. 'If any of the herders up on the sheilings catch us so much as touching the tree never mind picking mistletoe afore the ceremony, we'll both be boiled alive and served up with the mutton stew at the Samhain feast.'

'Don't worry, I'll no let anyone catch us, Jin.' Bram pulled out his own knife and nudged Tramper up to the edge of the wide stretch of grass where the sacred ground ended and the sheilings began. He weren't never going to use that blade on anyone, but I knew acting the brave warrior on this wee adventure were the only thrill he were going to get this Samhain now that he couldn't go hunting no more, so I kept my mouth shut and didn't laugh.

The mistletoe clumps that sprouted like giant bushes all over the oak were every bit as important to our tribe as the hallowed tree itself. I were glad there were some low-hanging branches thick with the green leaves and berries I could reach, as I weren't too keen on upsetting the spirits of the oak any further by clambering up to pick the mistletoe high up early. I were careful not to squash the big white berries as my blade sawed through the thick stems of each green twig, knowing if I did, I'd have a deal of bother getting the sticky sap off my hands again. After Samhain, Ma and some of the other woman would take the mistletoe off the village fence again and crush all the berries in big pots, spreading the thick glue on the branches of every tree they could find. Any bird no lucky enough to have flown off south afore now would find its wee feet stuck to the branch it landed on, and our village would have enough sparrow pie to see us through to the first snows of winter. My belly rumbled hungrily at the thought of the juicy stew and thick pastry crusts Ma would soon be making.

It weren't just Samhain feasting and tasty bird pie the hallowed tree reminded me of, though. It were wrapped up with way more memories than that. When I put my hand on the rough bark, I could hear my grandma's voice telling me the stories of how the tree had a heartbeat and the thick sap running through the branches were the lifeblood of our tribe. She said that the tree were thousands of summers old and its roots ran so deep, they fixed the tree to the centre of the whole world. Grandma were a bit like that – she were rooted deep in my memory. Though she were gone, it were like she were fixed somewhere deep inside me, and all I had to do were run a hand over the hallowed tree and smell the tang of its autumn leaves to see her face clear in my mind again, like she were standing afore me. I were only glad she'd no still been with us when I were told I were no fit for the Bairntime's Passing this year. The ceremony were held under the branches of our hallowed tree, and the thought of her eyes frowning at me from the knots in the oak's trunk made me shiver with shame.

I swallowed the resentment down and let my fingers trace the deep grooves in the gnarled bark, thinking on happier memories instead.

Pa would bring me and Bram here at the start of planting to offer a rabbit to the tree spirits and spread its blood on the bark to ask for a good crop. Pa always said that sacrifices had to be made for the things we want, so we sacrificed our meat at the outset, and we sacrificed our toil during the long, hard growing season. At the end of the season, we'd burn a sheaf of corn too, letting the scent drift up to the high branches and the ashes fall on the roots to nourish the oak. In summer, Ma would pick flowers with me to place under the tree to ask for health for the family and safety from danger. The bunches she picked this summer after Bram survived his accident near drowned the whole meadow round the tree with petals.

It were part of all of us, this tree. Even when I'd been bad and caused mischief and felt like the whole world were against me, I still had a refuge here. As long as I came and rested my head against the strong trunk and felt the life beating inside, I knew I were a Damnonii and I belonged, no matter what I did. I smiled as I cut the mistletoe stems and put each wee clump carefully into my leather pouch. I were going to fix the trouble I'd caused when I woke the stones, and everything were going to be alright.

I were so busy with the cutting, and Bram were so busy watching the sheilings to the north, we never saw what were coming over the grassland from the south till it were too late.

Chapter Sixteen

Felix

I only got a short head start on the demolition team.

Since the capture of the Damnonii slaves, the guards on top of the wall had been doubled and the sentries at the gate put on high alert. It wasn't until the gates were opened at mid-morning to let the builders drive their tool cart across the bridge that I got the chance to sneak out and run full pelt for the copse. Our Legate had marched to New Kilpatrick with his reinforcements at the crack of dawn – there was no one left at Caerpen Taloch who could put a stop to Brutus's plan. I knew for me to run ahead and warn the Damnonii what was coming would be seen as a traitorous act that might get me kicked out of the fort for good. But I couldn't keep my mouth shut about this and the slaves, not when it would start a war that could kill hundreds of people.

As soon as I reached the screen of trees, I looked back. Brutus and his soldiers were tramping across the bridge. He had three cohorts, a work team and a detachment of engineers – enough to cut down an entire forest and build a Roman fort in its place. But it wasn't a forest they were going to fell. It was just one tree.

They had to take the cart the long way around the copse and up to the meadow. On foot without equipment to slow me down, I could head straight up the slope and across the fields to Waterside village. I could only hope I could bring the Damnonii warriors back in time to stop the soldiers hacking the hallowed tree down. The tribespeople had been suspicious of me even before Bram's accident, but since that day, they'd treated me like I was diseased, shunning me if they came across me picking nuts or berries out past the wall. The only way I'd get them to believe this wasn't a trick was to find Bram. He'd believe me. Even after everything I'd done, Bram would know I was telling the truth.

My lungs were burning as I tore up the slope and into the meadow. I was so fixed on getting to the village I almost didn't notice there were two figures standing at the hallowed tree already. For a moment, my heart stopped, and I thought Brutus had somehow managed to get there ahead of me. Then I saw the figures were too short to be soldiers. They were dressed in tartan, and one was on a white pony.

'Bram! Jinny! Come quick!' I yelled, racing across the meadow and collapsing in a panting heap at the foot of the tree. 'The soldiers... coming... axes... chop down... have to tell... village...'

Jinny gripped her knife harder and glared at me like she was trying to work out which part to cut off first. Bram came trotting over quickly before she could start a fight, his eyes widening when he saw how out of breath with fear I was.

'Sheesh, Felix! What's amiss?'

Every moment I wasted trying to gulp down enough air to form a full sentence filled me with frustration, but finally I got enough breath back to gasp, 'The Romans are coming! They're going to chop down the hallowed tree! You have to get to the village and warn the warriors!'

'*WHAT?*' Jinny cried. 'They can't do that! Our tree's *sacred*!'

'They don't care. They're trying to start a war. There's no time to waste, you have to tell the village, right now!'

The panic in Jinny's eyes hardened into steel. 'Bram, race Tramper back and bring Gregor, Pa, and any of the folk who can wield a weapon – women and all if needs be.'

'But–'

'DO IT!'

Bram didn't need told twice. He could hear the thud of soldiers' boots on turf in the distance. He gave his pony a kick that told her he meant business, urging her into a gallop across the fields to his village. 'Don't do anything stupid, Jinny, promise!' he yelled over his shoulder as he raced away.

'How many are coming?' Jinny asked me, searching in her pockets to see if she had a weapon better than her short knife. All she came up with was a small sling.

'Almost fifty soldiers altogether. How many warriors are there at Waterside?'

'No more than a couple. Most of them are out hunting for the Samhain feast. The herders are up the sheiling and the folk that are left mind the farm. If we just had time to go to Torrance and Kinkell and some of the other villages to rouse folk there... Ach! Why'd you no come earlier to tell us, you rotten wee louse?'

'I did my best!' I spluttered. 'They'll kick me out for this, for sure.'

Jinny eyed me without much sympathy. 'Have you no brought a weapon?'

'Of course not! I'm trying to stop a war, not start one!'

'You're no help to anyone with one toe in the water and the other stuck on dry land!' Jinny growled. 'Either you're with us or you're no, which is it?'

'Er...'

'Right, you're with us then. Here, take this, grab a pile of rocks, and lob 'em at anything that looks even halfways like a metal man.'

I took the catapult she thrust at me and hunted around for loose stones, hoping the villagers would get here in time and I wouldn't have to use it. I didn't think I'd stand much chance against Brutus and a detachment of his best soldiers with a handful of pebbles and a strip of leather I wasn't entirely sure I knew how to use. It might've been almost funny if my weapon hadn't been the same sling Jinny had used to nearly knock my head off only a few days before.

'That's them here now.' Jinny nodded at the line of soldiers appearing at the far side of the meadow and licked her lips nervously. We looked back towards the village in the distance. We couldn't see Bram anymore, and we couldn't see a mob of angry villagers charging to the rescue either. This was going to be a close-run thing. Jinny put her hand on the ancient tree's trunk and stroked it protectively. 'I'm no going to let them so much as put a dent in you,' she whispered. 'I promise.'

I didn't want to tell her she shouldn't make promises she had no way of keeping. I was pretty sure she knew that already.

I could see the sun glinting off the soldiers' armour now, and the whites of the horse's eyes as it pulled on the cart harness. Septicus Strabo, the Standard Bearer, marched alongside with his face set hard, holding the legion's eagle up proudly. They'd set out to strike fear into the hearts of the villagers and no mistake. The magnificent golden bird sat atop its pole with its wings outstretched to the sky, and all the power and might of Rome seemed to blaze from that glittering standard, setting our hearts pounding with awe and dread.

There was a swagger in the Senior Centurion's step as he led them towards the hallowed tree. He only stopped when he was close enough to make out that one of the two figures standing against the trunk and waving a makeshift weapon wasn't wearing tartan.

'Marcus Lucius Aquila!' Brutus yelled, hurling my given name at me like it was a curse. 'What in the name of Jupiter are you doing here? Get away from that tree this instant or I'll have you flogged, boy!'

I held my ground, despite my legs shaking so badly I could barely stand. 'I'm not going anywhere, Brutus,' I said as bravely as I could. 'Our Legate said we weren't to do anything to anger the Damnonii. I'm only following his orders.'

'Since when is selling your own kind out to the savages following the Commander's orders?' Brutus snapped, looking across the fields and seeing something that made him grind his teeth with rage. I risked taking my eyes off Brutus for a quick glance back, my heart leaping in hope when I saw a crowd of villagers running our way over the fields.

'I'm doing this *because* I'm a loyal Roman,' I said, the sight of the tribesfolk giving me courage. 'If you want to kill me for doing my duty then go ahead.'

'I'm not going to kill you on purpose, boy,' Brutus growled, drawing his sword. 'But if you get in the way of my workers, well... that's your problem.' He nodded at the team of soldiers carrying axes and sledgehammers. They advanced towards us menacingly, with no intention of letting a half-blood Roman boy and a Damnonii girl get in the way of their work. Jinny grabbed my hand and squeezed it. I wasn't sure if she was looking for reassurance or telling me to get ready for a fight, but I squeezed it back anyway and raised my sling.

Before the soldiers reached the tree, an arrow came whistling through the air, landing in the ground a hand-span in front of one of the axemen. The team stopped, looking back at Brutus for orders. He motioned for them to halt, yelling at the rest of the soldiers to get into formation and advance with their shields up.

Just then the villagers arrived in full force, circling the tree and waving their collection of makeshift weapons angrily at the Romans. It was mostly farmers with picks, women with spades and hoes and older children with short knives, but they made me feel a bit safer despite their lack of real armaments. Only a small band of them standing in front of me and Jinny had real weapons. Gregor, the village head, had a broad sword, and Jinny's father, Donall, riding Bram's pony, had a long, polished blade. The blacksmith had a fierce-looking axe, and two other men both had bows with a quiver full of arrows each. It was never going to be enough.

'Get off our land!' Gregor thundered. 'Or we'll send you running back to that wall of yours with less arms and legs than when you started the day!'

Brutus ignored him, not even bothering to ask me for a translation. 'Men, advance!' he ordered. 'Cut down anyone in your path.'

'They're no going to listen to reason, Gregor,' Donall said through gritted teeth. 'If we're to save this tree, we'll need to hold the ground.'

'Agreed. Bairns, stay at the back of the group behind the women,' Gregor ordered. 'You're only to join the fight if the rest of us can't keep the tree defended. That means you too, Jinny.'

'I'm no going nowhere.' I could feel Jinny trembling beside me, but her eyes were narrowed and she kept a tight hold of her knife, facing the Romans without flinching. No one was going to back down. This was about to get ugly.

'Wait!' I shouted in Latin, running out and standing in front of the advancing soldiers. 'This is against our Legate's orders!'

'We're following our Senior Centurion's orders, that's good enough for us,' the Standard Bearer snarled at me. 'Out of the way, boy, before you're trampled down.'

'But our Legate said we've to keep the peace!'

'Romans don't make peace with savages! Now *move*!' The Standard Bearer raised his eagle, ready to strike me with the heavy pole. So I did the only thing I could think of to stop the advancing soldiers. I grabbed the eagle standard and made off with it, running full pelt across the meadow towards the sacred valley.

I only got halfway there before the blade that Brutus threw tore through my tunic. Even from a distance, the Senior Centurion's aim was perfect. It was like being kicked in the back by a carthorse. The knife lodged between my shoulder blades, sending me sprawling to the grass with my head spinning. I tried to get back up, but none of my limbs were listening anymore. The whole world swam out of focus, and the last thing I saw clearly as I lay with my face in the grass was the Standards Bearer's boots as he ran over to retrieve the legion's eagle.

The sounds that came next all bled together in a chaos of noise and confusion. The Damnonii villagers yelling, Brutus shouting orders, the clang of picks and hoes off the soldiers' metal shields, screams and howls of pain and fear... Then everything went dark.

For a long time, it was as though the world didn't even exist.

When I finally opened my eyes again, my head was throbbing, my whole body was numb, and sun had changed position in the sky. I tried to roll over to escape the raw sawing noise that grated on my ears. But I couldn't move. I was too weak to even cry out for help. I couldn't hear the cry of the villagers anymore, or the clash of weapons. The only sound was the great buzz of noise that scraped back and forth between my eardrums. As I lost my fight to stay conscious and the darkness closed in again, I finally worked out what I was hearing.

It was the sound of a huge Roman saw on the trunk of a tree.

Chapter Seventeen

Jinny

I'd no cried this much since the day of Bram's accident and Raggy's death.

After the fight, there were chaos in the village, folks lugging home injured men, women and bairns between them and running for herbs and clean cloths to patch up their wounds. We'd had to abandon the hallowed tree to the metal men to save ourselves in the end, and the wailing that went up when we heard it crashing to the ground were enough to wake the dead in their graves. When the other Damnonii from Torrance, Kinkell, Harestanes and all the settlements within riding distance of Waterside heard about the tree, our village were swamped with angry tribesfolk all weeping and yelling and vowing revenge.

It weren't until the sun started to set and we'd done as much for the wounded as could be, that the tears dried up and the Elders of the villages met to decide what to do next. Even though they shut themselves up in the Council hut and talked in hushed voices, none of us needed to eavesdrop to know what the decision would be. We'd be going to war with the Romans now, no doubt about it. Even without Gregor to lead us, our village would fight to the death to avenge what we'd lost.

Our village chief were sore wounded. That big sword of his had clobbered half a dozen metal men afore he got run through the side with a spear. The other men at the front of the battle hadn't fared much better. Calan, the blacksmith, had his face split near in two with a Roman axe. One of the archers got killed, and it were a miracle my pa escaped without more than a torn shoulder and a deep gash to the thigh. All told, five men and two women lay dead by sundown, and a bairn no older than eight springs were still trying to make up his mind whether to stay or pass on.

When the hush of evening fell on our village, I sat in our hut with Ma and Bram, stirring the pot with fresh bandages that were boiling over the fire, and playing with the food in my bowl instead of eating it. I were weary with weeping over the dead and wounded, weighed down with grief over the hallowed tree, and sick with worry about Pa. Since Gregor were half dead and no able to open his eyes never mind lead us, Ailsa were acting as village chief and Pa were invited to the Council meeting to make up the numbers. I knew he'd be an Elder one day, I just didn't expect the time to come so soon. Somehow, my pa being one of them who would vote to send the men and women of our village to their certain deaths against the metal men made the whole thing seem even worse.

'Jinny, careful with that, you'll have the whole pot tipped over into the fire!' Ma snapped, grabbing the spoon off me and taking the bubbling pot off the boil. 'I asked you to hang them strips up to dry an age ago, can you no just do as you're told?'

I mumbled an apology, but for once, I didn't answer back. I knew Ma weren't mad at me, but at the metal men and their wickedness. She were even more afeared of what were to come than I were, what with two bairns to lose and the kiss of death brushing so close to her youngest she could almost taste it.

'You alright, Bram? You want me to get you some more stew?' I asked. 'There's a wee gob left in the pan.'

'Not hungry,' Bram shrugged, sitting on the floor with his good leg stretched out in front of him and picking at the stew in his bowl like I'd served him up a feast of maggots.

When he'd gone back to warn the village earlier, Pa had taken Tramper off him and told him to stay in our hut till it were all over. After the fight when we'd got halfway home with the wounded, we'd found Bram crawling through the fields to get to us. He'd hopped as far as he could until his leg gave out, then he'd gritted his teeth and pulled himself along with his one good hand. After the confusion of running about with bandages and boiling water for the healer, I'd found Bram back in our hut staring at the wall with a blank look on his face. He weren't even crying at what had happened. At first I thought he were mad at being left behind, then I realised it were worse than that. He'd given up hope of ever being any use to anyone, and he were sinking into himself like snow melting in a spring thaw. It frightened me even more than the threat of war.

'Bram, come on, you've got to eat something. Just a wee taste, hmm? There's going to be a lot of going back and forth to the villages tomorrow to organise things, and you and Tramper will be needed to carry important messages and suchlike. Your wee pony made it out of the fight in one piece at least.'

'There's plenty of folk to do that, Jin,' Bram sighed. 'They'll no be needing me. What use will I be? You'll all go off to war with the Romans and I'll just be sitting here by the fire waiting for the corpses to be carried home. Maybe you'll all die and there'll no even be anyone left to do the fetching.'

'Don't say such things!' I said, glancing up to make sure Ma were busy with her poultice preparations and no listening to us. 'We'll all have a part to play – you and all. It's a leg you're missing, no a brain. Anyhow, after today, the Council will no let the bairns of the village near the metal men again, so put all them thoughts of fighting a war out of your head.'

My wee brother sighed again. He sounded so cast down with sorrow it were worse than seeing tears.

'Don't fret, Bram. The tree can't be helped now and we've done our best for the dead and wounded. There's nothing can be fixed by breaking our hearts with sadness.'

It were something our grandma used to say to me whenever I came running to her crying about the unfairness of the world. She knew whatever punishment I'd got had no doubt been earned by my own mischief, but she always gave me a hug and made me feel better. I hugged Bram now, feeling his bony wee shoulders trembling in my arms and his breath all choked up in his throat. If he kept this up, he'd make himself sick with fretting.

'C'mon, you wee daftie, tell me what's eating you up or I'll fetch a bucket of slops from the pig farm and flush your secrets out of you faster than a dose of the healer's salts.'

Bram half smiled at that, then sighed again. 'It's no just the tree and the death and suffering, though that's enough to keep us all awake for a lifetime,' he said softly. 'Jin, I were wondering... is it true what they're saying? About Felix?'

'What are they saying?' I bristled at the mention of the

Roman boy's name.

'Some of the bairns who were there and saw it all said he were the one who made sure the villagers were gathered at the tree so the Romans could attack them. They said as soon as he'd done his job and the fight had started, he ran away laughing back to the fort.'

'That weren't what happened,' I frowned.

'Then what did happen? Were Felix really just scheming with the Romans the whole time?'

'I don't... I'm no...' I started, then stopped. The lead-up to the fight and the whole awful battle were just a blur in my mind. The only things I remembered clearly were Felix squeezing my hand when we caught sight of the soldiers and the look of fear in his eyes when the men with axes advanced. The rest of my thoughts were all splintered with panic and echoing with the screams of the villagers.

'I don't know why he ran, Bram. Maybe he were just as afeared as the rest of us.'

'So you don't think he were helping the Romans? You think he really were on our side?'

I struggled to answer that. I wanted to believe so badly that the Roman boy were rotten to the core and the cause of all our troubles, it hurt to admit the truth. But I'd had enough of the bitter taste of spite I'd been carrying around in my mouth for so long, and I finally spat it out. 'Aye, I think he were helping us. Else he wouldn't have been afeared of the soldiers, would he? But Bram, I think...' I paused, another memory flashing into my head.

'What, Jin?'

'I think Felix might've got hurt in the fight. When he ran away, just as the soldiers were about to charge, I saw him run off with their big golden pole.'

'Golden pole? What's that?' Bram looked confused.

'You know, the one with a big bird on the top with outstretched wings?'

'I've never seen it, Jin.'

'Me neither afore today, I heard about it from Calan, the blacksmith. Some time back, he were telling stories of the war afore the building of the wall, and he said the pole with the bird were important to the metal men. Anyhow, I think the soldiers might've hurt Felix to get it back. I'm awful sure I saw a knife in the air and him falling in the grass just afore the metal men attacked.'

'You mean he could be lying dead up in the meadow for helping us?' Bram's eyes widened till they near popped out his head. It weren't much of a job I were doing of making him feel better.

'Don't fret, Bram! I'm sure the Romans'll take care of him. They've got their own healers and herbs in that big fort of theirs.'

'But they'll no want nothing to do with him now they know he warned us they were coming and helped us try to save the tree!' Bram insisted. 'We have to go and look for him, Jin, we have to help him!'

'Ssh! Keep your voice down, Bram!' I hissed as Ma came back in after giving her poultices to the healer. She threw us a questioning look, but she were too busy with preparing the bandages to pay us much mind. I waited till she bent over the wee table again to say, 'Bram, you know you can't go out tonight. Pa will have a fit if he comes back to find you gone. I have to slip out of the village just now anyhow, so I'll look out for Felix while I'm gone.'

'Gone?' Bram blinked. 'Gone where?'

'Where d'you think, you wee daftie? I have to go to the sacred circle, remember?'

'You're no still fussing over the stones after everything that's happened, Jin? It's the metal men we need to be worrying about.'

'The Romans are no the ones walking the fields and sheilings at night carrying folk off to feast on!' I said. 'Look, Bram, it were my fault they got woken up, and it's my job to put them back to sleep, so–'

'Your fault? You said it were all down to Felix!'

'Well... thing is... both of us sort of had a hand in it. Anyhow,' I hurried on, 'there'll be folks traipsing back and forth between the villages and spreading news tonight, and no doubt a whole group up at the tree stump mourning over the loss, so if I don't get the mistletoe spread round the circle, then the stones'll have a whole banquet of folk to choose from.'

'You still got the bag of mistletoe from earlier?' Bram asked.

I patted the pouch I carried over my shoulder. 'I have to go now afore the stones wake. You understand why I can't take you with me this time, Bram, don't you? I can slip out on my own and be back afore anyone misses me, but if I take you and Tramper, we're bound to be spotted. This job's too important to take the risk.'

'Understanding something's no the same as liking it,' Bram grumbled, but he knew I'd never stop him from running out with me unless the reason were a good one. 'I'll just sit here and be useless till you get back, then.'

'You'll no be useless, Bram,' I snorted. 'You'll be out

with the other bairns, eavesdropping on the Council and tapping the Samhain cider barrels as soon as my back's turned.'

Bram smiled properly for the first time at that. We both knew he wouldn't leave the hut till I got back, but it made us both feel better to pretend he'd be up to his usual tricks given half the chance.

'Make sure Ma don't suspect nothing, and cover for me if Pa gets back afore me,' I whispered. Bram nodded and squeezed my arm for luck, then I got up and said as careless as I could to Ma, 'I've got to go and help Coira and Mairi with their pa. He got right scraped up with the Roman swords today.'

'The healer's got it in hand, Jinny, what do they need your help for?' Ma looked up from the bandages she were hanging on the drying rack above the fire.

'No with their pa, I mean with the cooking,' I said quickly. 'What with them and their ma being so caught up with things, they'll have no one to put on a pot of stew.'

'That's kind of you, Jinny, you're a good lass,' Ma smiled.

I smiled back through a guilty mask and hurried out, wondering how come the only time I ever got praised were for something I weren't going to do.

It were easier than I'd supposed to slip out of the village unseen.

Although the hunters were back and madder than the four winds in winter at what had taken place while they were gone, it were the metal men they were watching for, no wee lassies like me. They had to keep the gates open as there were still folk coming in from the other villages to help with the wounded and the war preparations. No one paid me no mind, no even when I tiptoed past the guards at the gate and disappeared off across the fields.

The moon were hidden and the clouds were thick with gathered rain, like the sky were ready to burst with sorrow over what had happened to our hallowed tree. I could almost feel the anger of the spirits whipping the wind and rumbling with thunder in the distance. There were a storm coming and the night were full of brooding and menace. I could only hope the stones were no awake yet as I hurried down the valley pass and slipped into the mist.

I were so scared I couldn't hardly hear the boom of thunder over the pounding of my heart. It were so dark I could scarce make out my own two feet, and I wished I'd had the forethought to bring a lantern with me. It couldn't be helped now. I'd just have to be careful no to walk slap bang into the stones in the gloom.

I heard the whistling afore I saw them.

It were no the wind nor the thunder that were making the uncanny tune that rose and fell on the air. It were like the stones were mocking me, throwing the song that had woken them back in my face with each fresh stirring of the mist. As soon as I heard it start up, I near dropped my bag of mistletoe and went running for home with my legs all shaking like I'd got the palsy. But I couldn't do that. No when more folk were in danger of being hurt by the mischief I'd caused. So instead, I clapped my hands to my ears so I couldn't hear the whistling of the wind and walked right on until I came to the stone circle itself.

I could see them moving now.

No up and walking exactly, but the dark shadows of the great stones were shuddering and shaking in the mist like they were stirring themselves ready to walk the night. I tried not to look, grabbing a handful of mistletoe and keeping my mind on spreading it round the ground just outside the circle of stones. My hands were shaking so hard with the fear of them waking giants I kept dropping the leaves, wasting precious time picking them up and putting them in the right place as the whistling got louder and louder.

Almost there, Jinny, I told myself, trying to keep from freezing up with fear. *Just this last wee bit then you're done, and they can't get out and come for you...*

I were so focused on my task, so bent on getting the mistletoe spread and the stones trapped inside their circle, that I didn't see the thing creeping out of the mist behind me.

Chapter Eighteen

Felix

I couldn't see anything. The whole world was dark and there was a weird piping sound in my ears as though the wind was whistling a strange, distorted tune. I stumbled on, my body numb and my mind fuzzy, focused only on finding shelter before the storm broke. I could feel it gathering in the air above me, the rainclouds ready to burst and soak me to the skin. Beads of sweat gathered on my forehead, and my back felt like there was a shard of ice buried between my shoulder blades. If I didn't get out of the open and under cover soon, I wasn't going to last the night. I had to get back to the fort and beg them to let me in before the last of my strength gave out.

My feet crunched over something soft that popped and squelched beneath my boots. I looked down, and through the swirling mist, I could just make out piles of green leaves and white berries laid out in a rough circle. When I looked back up again, I groaned in dismay. Instead of heading through the copse like I'd hoped, I'd blundered down into the valley where the stone giants lay in wait. Huge shadows loomed above me in the dark, faces in the rock fading in and out of the mist. I couldn't be sure in my confused state, but it seemed as though eyes were opening in the stone and turning to glare at me.

The giants were awake.

Then suddenly, one of them started moving, lumbering through the mist towards me with arms outstretched and wild hair streaming in the wind.

Wait, wild hair...?

Somehow that didn't seem right, but it wasn't until I heard a frightened yell and I collided with a warm body wrapped in a tartan shawl that I realised I wasn't being stalked by the stone giants after all.

'Jinny! What are you doing here?' I gasped. At least, that's what I tried to say, but all that came out was a long groan as I collapsed onto my knees.

Everything that happened next was a confused blur.

I babbled something about getting out of the valley quickly as the stones were waking, and Jinny said something about mistletoe, which made no sense at all. When she grabbed me under the arms and helped me walk, there were flashes of intense pain in my shoulder as I stumbled along, and moments when everything went black. Then there was the sound of a door closing and the wind died, the rolling clouds disappearing. When the world came back into focus, I found myself lying in a pile of straw on a wooden floor wrapped in Jinny's tartan shawl.

'I've taken the knife out,' she said, her voice sounding like it was coming from somewhere in the far distance. 'And I've patched up the hole as best I can. It's no as bad or as deep as it looks, but you'll need to stay still and sleep for a while afore you can risk moving again.'

Sleep. *Yes.* That was the best thing I'd heard all day.

'I'll be back in the morning. Don't go anywhere till I get here, alright?'

I didn't have the strength to tell her I couldn't go anywhere even if I wanted to. The door closed again, and I drifted into a deep sleep filled with falling trees and flying axes and great big stone mouths that opened in the mist and swallowed me whole.

In the early hours of the morning, the storm broke, the rain battering off the low roof above me and searching for cracks in the walls. I was too exhausted to care if it found a way in and I drowned in my sleep, just as long as I didn't have to get up from my warm bed of straw and wool ever again. It wasn't until the sunshine streaming through the open door woke me that I realised how long I'd been asleep. Jinny had returned like she'd promised, and better still, she'd brought me a fat pigkin bladder filled with warm stew.

'Careful!' she warned as I sat up too fast and nearly choked myself trying to swallow it down. 'You'll no get better with your lungs filled with mutton and turnip.'

'Hungry,' I mumbled between mouthfuls. 'Where am I?'

'One of the herder's huts at the edge of the sheiling. They mainly just use them at calfing, so no one'll come near at this time of year. And now that I've sent the stones back to sleep with the mistletoe, you'll be safe from them stone giants at night and all.'

Jinny looked so proud at what she'd done that I didn't have the heart to tell her it was all for nothing and the Romans were behind the vanishings. I'd betrayed my own people enough already. 'Does anyone know I'm here?' I asked instead.

'Just Bram. He's been on at me to let him come and see you, but right now it's too dangerous.'

'Why? Are the Romans patrolling north of the wall?' My heart skipped a beat at the thought of being caught. I'd been ready to throw myself on their mercy last night when

I was desperate, but now I was feeling a bit stronger, the thought of Brutus and his soldiers getting hold of me after what I'd done sent shivers down my spine. I tried to get to my feet and look out of the door, but Jinny pushed me back down again.

'Stay still, you've got a ways to go yet till you're healed. Here, I brought some of Ma's poultices and bandages, they'll have that wee cut healed up in no time.'

She changed the dressing on my back, and from the way it stung and my vision blurred, I was pretty sure it was way worse than just a 'wee cut'. I bit my tongue, though, trying not to cry out and look like a coward. I didn't want her reminding me about the wounds Bram had suffered at the hands of the Romans and how brave he'd been about it all. When she was finished, I asked again, 'So, why did you say it's "dangerous" for me here if the soldiers haven't been seen beyond the wall since yesterday?'

'Ach, Felix, it's no the metal men I'm talking about, it's...'

'Who?'

'Well... Folks at the village are no too happy about what you did down on the meadow the other day.'

'What I did?' I blinked in confusion. 'But I tried to help you, Jinny!'

'I know that, and Bram knows that of course,' she shrugged, 'but other folks see it different. The way they look at it, you lured them to the tree so the Romans could take a shot at them, then you went running off as soon as the swords were drawn.'

I was too angry now to stay lying down any longer. 'I betrayed my own people to try to stop them cutting your sacred tree down!' I yelled, sitting up and throwing the shawl back at Jinny. 'I was trying to stop a war that would get lots of you killed! Now I'll never be allowed to go home! I'll be stuck out here on my own when the Romans leave, and instead of thanks, you lot just talk about me behind my back like I'm some kind of monster! It's not fair!'

My head swam and I had to close my eyes and rest against the wall so I didn't pass out. When I'd caught my breath and opened them again, Jinny was giving me a strange look, like she was seeing me for the very first time.

'You know, up till now, my mind weren't made up on whose side you were taking in our tribe's fight with the Romans who have taken our land,' she frowned. 'Me and Bram have been arguing over you since the spring, and it's no easy thinking different of you now.'

'Then why are you helping me?' I muttered.

''Cause I promised Bram I would.'

'Oh. Is that all?'

'You're no what I thought you were, Felix, that's for sure,' she frowned. 'But what with you speaking up for the metal men after Bram's accident, and now looking like you were part of that wicked plan to cut our tree down and get tribesfolk killed, well... you'll no be looked on too kindly if you're seen this side of the wall again. You'll need to be careful from now on.'

I was half aware that Jinny's words stung like fresh knife wounds, but I was too weak to fight back. I lay down on the straw again and turned my face to the wall, wishing now I'd just stayed in the fort and left Brutus and the soldiers to get on with hacking down the tree without interfering. I hadn't stopped their plan to start a war, and now I wasn't welcome on either side of the wall. Everything I'd done had been for nothing.

Jinny sat with me for a bit longer trying to get me to drink more water and have some more stew, but she finally left me to it when she saw I wasn't in the mood to do more than sulk and sleep. When the door closed behind her, the silence seemed to fill every corner of the empty hut, and I wished I had the strength to get up and call her back. Instead I fell into an uneasy sleep, tossing and turning and longing for my father to come and find me and tell me everything was going to be alright.

When I woke again and saw the long shadows of evening cast on the walls, the loneliness ached even more than the knife wound in my back. I got up and went to the door, peering out at the sunset and wondering what I was going to do now. For the first time ever, the sight of Jinny stomping over the fields towards me made me almost dizzy with relief. 'You came back!' I called, trying not to grin too widely.

'I said I would, didn't I? I'm no a liar. No all the time, anyhow.'

She checked to make sure there was no one else in sight, then ducked into the hut to join me. My mouth watered at the delicious smell coming from her basket, and I could hardly believe my eyes when she uncovered a hunk of roast beef, a half wheel of cheese and a crusty loaf fresh from the oven.

'Don't go thinking we get to feast on the likes of this grub every day of the year,' she warned as I made a grab for the meat. 'It's only 'cause of the Samhain festival being put off on account of the coming war. Our village has near been swamped by warriors flooding in from every corner of the land, ready for a fight with the metal men.'

'Is Bram making you feed me or did you come because you wanted to?' I couldn't help asking with my mouth full of food.

'He said if I didn't bring you supper he'd fill my bedroll with Tramper's dung and make me sleep in it,' Jinny shrugged. 'But I guess I weren't averse to the chance of getting out of the village for a bit, what with all the tension and talk of war.'

I swallowed hard and put the bread down, my appetite suddenly disappearing. 'So it's worked then? The soldiers' plan, I mean? The Damnonii are definitely going to war with the Romans?'

'What choice have we got?' Jinny growled. 'They've taken something more precious to us than the air we breathe, and they've killed more than half a dozen good people going about it.'

'That's not all they've taken,' I said, making up my mind to tell Jinny everything I knew. She was risking a whole lot of trouble on my account, and there didn't seem much point in keeping secrets for the Romans anymore.

'What do you mean by that?'

'You remember the sleeping stones, and how you threw that rock and we both thought they'd been woken up, and–'

'Look, can we no just let that lie?' Jinny grumbled. 'You were a wee maggot and gave Bram's secret away, I were a bit too eager to get even, and neither of us can claim we don't have some share of the blame. Let's just leave it at that and no go remembering things that can't be helped now.'

It took me a moment to work out that Jinny was apologising.

'Then you don't blame me for Bram's accident?' I asked hopefully.

Jinny screwed her face up like she was fighting a war with her own mind. Finally, she said, 'I wanted to. I wanted it to be your fault so bad I near tore myself in two with hating you. But truth be told, if I'd no been shirking my chores that day and if I'd no talked Bram into hunting rabbits with me instead of minding the sheep like he were supposed to, we never would've been in that copse in the first place. It's my fault what happened to Bram, no one else's.'

'It's not your fault, Jinny. It was just an accident.' I put my hand on her arm when I saw a big tear slide down her face. She brushed it off and shook my hand away angrily.

'It's no pity I'm looking for, Roman boy. It's a way to put things right.'

'That's what I want too!' I said, 'but I don't know how. And I wasn't going to blame you for waking the stones, I just wanted you to know it's all just a story. You didn't wake them that day in the circle. We've just been imagining them moving in the mist.'

'Yes, I did,' Jinny frowned. 'I know that were what I did. Four people have vanished clean off the face of the earth, and it's them stones that have gobbled them up.'

'No, that was the Romans,' I told her. 'They took those four people and locked them up in the fort. They're keeping them as slaves.'

'WHAT?' Jinny jumped up so fast she upset the basket, and the cheese went rolling across the floor. 'I have to get back to the village and tell Ailsa her Conner's still alive and them nasty metal men have got him! I have to–'

'Jinny, wait a minute!' I grabbed her arm again and pulled her back. 'We're trying to think of a way to stop the war, remember? If you tell everyone the Romans have taken Damnonii slaves, then it'll just make everyone even more determined to fight. The Romans are too strong – they'll slaughter every single person who comes within half a mile of the wall.'

'Our Damnonii warriors are every bit as good as your metal men, and no afraid of the taste of raw steel!' Jinny snapped. 'They'll no run from a fight just 'cause the Romans are hiding behind a stupid pile of turf and a daft wee line of sticks. No like you, taking to your heels the other day like you were going to pee yourself on the spot if you stayed.'

'I wasn't running because I was scared!' I protested.

'No? That were what it looked like.'

'I was trying to stop the Romans from attacking the villagers, stupid.'

'By running away? Great plan, Roman boy, well done you.'

'Shut up and listen for a minute!' I yelled, totally exasperated now. 'I was trying to steal the legion's standard – you know, the pole with the eagle on it? The legion can't go into battle without it. I thought if I could run far enough away with it, then by the time the Romans caught me and got it back, the Damnonii would be able to gather all your warriors together to protect your tree.'

Jinny thought about it for a bit, then nodded. 'Hmph, that weren't such a bad idea after all,' she admitted. 'Pity you run like a three-legged goat, or we'd have stood a better chance of keeping our tree.'

'It doesn't matter now,' I sighed. 'It was all for nothing. The tree's gone, people are dead, the Romans have got a group of Damnonii slaves, and no matter what we do, there's going to be a war that'll kill half the tribespeople in the land. If only we could think of a way to delay the war, just for a few days.'

'What good would that do? Folks'll still get killed in the end,' Jinny scowled.

'No, they won't,' I said. 'Our Commander said orders were coming from Rome for the legions to abandon the wall and head back south. It's become too expensive, and our leaders in Rome think it's a waste of money defending a land that nobody cares about from a band of savages nobody wants as slaves. Those Damnonii in the fort won't do as they're told unless they've got three soldiers each guarding them. Even Brutus thinks they're a bigger headache than they're worth, and it was his idea in the first place.'

'You mean to say them metal men are causing all this trouble over our land, and they don't even want to stay?' Jinny looked like she was close to exploding. 'The wicked–'

'It's our leaders in Rome who want us to fall back south to Hadrian's Wall,' I said quickly. 'But some of the senior soldiers at Caerpen Taloch want to stay here. If they can stir up a war with the locals, there'll be a chance for honours and promotions, and being in charge of their own fort up here gives them far better standing in the army than sharing one with several other southern legions.'

'So if we can just think of a way of stopping the Damnonii from attacking the wall, or the metal men from coming out from behind it for a wee while, then the Romans'll have to march off again and nobody needs to get killed?'

'Yes, that's it exactly. Um... any ideas?'

There was silence for a long moment, then Jinny's eyes lit up and she grinned from ear to ear. 'Aye, I got one. Only truth be told, it were your idea, no mine.'

'My idea? What do you... Oh.' It slowly dawned on me what we needed to do. If I'd thought warning the Damnonii about the soldiers coming to cut down the tree was a betrayal so treacherous I'd never be allowed back in the fort again, then this would be the death of any hope I'd ever have of joining the Roman army and becoming a soldier. It was an act of such awful treason that even my own father would disown me if he knew what I was planning.

But I didn't have a choice. A war was coming, and if I didn't help Jinny and the other villagers, then their blood would be on my hands.

Damnonii blood.

My mother's blood.

My blood.

Chapter Nineteen

Jinny

If I'd thought the hardest part of the plan would be slipping out of the village in the dead of night with the gates locked and the warriors all on high alert, I were dead wrong.

The hardest part were getting away without Bram making a fuss.

'But why can't I come with you, Jinny?' he asked for about the eighty-seventh time as I were packing my kit bag with rope and a hunting knife and anything else I could think of that might come in handy when we went sneaking into the fort.

'We've been over this already, Bram,' I sighed, setting my bag down and giving Tramper a wee pat to settle her down. She could sense Bram's fidgets, and she were snorting and stamping, ready to throw him if he weren't careful. 'I need you here to cause a big ruckus at the other end of the village to give me a chance to slip out unseen. I can't do it without you, Bram, it's too important a job to leave to any of the wee bairns.'

It were the night of Samhain, and instead of being full of feasting tribesfolk, our village were packed with every warrior from one end of the land to the other, all waiting for the dawn to rise on their day of battle. Pa and the Elders of all the other villages were marching around making sure the weapons were sharp and the archers and swordsmen all knew their orders. The tension were drawn so tight, the very night air felt close to snapping. I had one shot to get that Roman eagle and put a stop to the war tomorrow, and I weren't going to manage it if I couldn't even get out of the village unseen in the first place.

'Every job I've ever been given since that cursed accident has been "stay in the village, Bram; mind the chickens, Bram; stir the pot, Bram; sit on your bum, Bram, and don't do nothing that a bairn of five summers couldn't do". I'm sick of it, Jin! I need some adventure, or I'll go plumb mad!'

'This is no a rabbit hunt, Bram!' I snapped, making Tramper flinch. 'This is life and death, and your job here is every bit as important as mine. Besides, it's going to be hard enough just me and Felix sneaking up on the wall unseen. You really think the metal men are so blind they couldn't spot a lad on a white horse coming at them out the moonlight?'

'Ach, I know, Jin, it's just... I'm so sick of feeling useless all the time.' Bram sighed, nudging Tramper into a walk round the barn to keep her from stamping and disturbing the other horses. 'I'm afeared I'll be stuck in the village for the rest of my life doing daft wee chores while everyone looks on me like I'm a helpless wee cripple. I want a chance to prove my worth, to show them all I can still hunt deer and wield a knife and bring home rabbits like I used to.'

'I know, Bram, I know,' I gulped, a big lump of sadness in my throat. 'I'm longing for a chance to show them I'm no a wee bairn too, that I'm every bit as good as the new-made women. But if I'm caught sneaking out of the village and into the Roman fort on the eve of war, it'll just prove to the Council I can't be trusted never again. But this is no about us and what we want. Do you no see? This is about making sure our people are safe and don't have to get killed in some stupid fight they can't win.'

Bram looked doubtful. He weren't mad keen when he first heard my plan, and that were afore I told him he'd have to stay in the village if he wanted to help us. 'I still don't see how the Council will put a stop to the war even if you do bring that big pole with the eagle back here,' he grumbled. 'Seems to me, they'll just think it's an even better reason to fight.'

'Ach, Bram, have you no been listening? The Romans have Connor and the other three folk who vanished. They're due to go marching south any time now, and they'll no give them villagers back, no now they've turned them into slaves. Ailsa and the other Elders are no stupid, they don't want this war no more than you nor me. If I can give them a chance to bargain the slaves back, then maybe it'll give them a reason no to go to war.'

'But what about avenging the hallowed tree and the folks them metal men killed the other day?' Bram said. 'I can't see the Council just forgetting about that.'

'If there's one thing I've learned these last few seasons, Bram,' I said, slinging my bag on my shoulder and making sure my wee knife were safe in my pocket, 'it's that holding a grudge and taking revenge don't hurt no one but yourself in the end. The Elders are smart enough to know that themselves already. They'll choose the path of peace if I can just bring them a way of doing it without making us all look like cowards.'

'I hope you're right, Jin.'

'Aye, me too.'

'Is that you all set then?'

'Ready and waiting for your signal.'

'Alright then. Good luck, Jinny.'

'You too, you wee daftie.'

Bram grinned at me and turned Tramper out of the barn, heading for the north end of the village where the cows and sheep had been herded down from the sheiling and fenced into pens to keep them safe in case the fighting spread out north of the wall. Winter were on its way, and if the war lasted more than a short time, we couldn't risk being caught without supplies to hand. They were making a right noise of mooing and lowing, but that were nothing compared to the noise they'd be making as soon as Bram got to work.

I skirted the barns and milking sheds, trying to keep to the shadows and no draw attention to myself. The warriors were all gathered round the blacksmith's workshop, getting their swords and axes sharpened and their shields hammered into shape. A whole crowd of womenfolk from different villages were sewing the leather straps of the armour together, the tougher ones gearing themselves up for the fight too. We needed every strong-armed warrior we could find to send up the wall, and the Damnonii were no too fussed who joined the fight, as long as they were able to wield an axe or throw a spear.

Even though the place were full to bursting and folk were working so hard that sweat were pouring from their brows, the village were strangely silent, like the night were holding its breath. It weren't just for fear of the Romans neither. Tonight were Samhain, and for the first time ever, we had no mistletoe hung round the village to protect us. The door to the spirit world were wide open, and there weren't no way to stop the spirits walking right through and coming to hunt us. It made me shiver just thinking about it.

I'd almost made it past the Council hut without being seen, when a hand clamped down on my shoulder and I were spun around like a wee top.

'Jinny! Should you no be in your bed by now, lass?'

I looked up to see Pa frowning down at me, and gulped hard. 'I'm just running up to the herb beds to get some rosemary and thyme for Ma's poultices, then I'll go straight to sleep, promise,' I lied, hoping the grin I gave him looked honest instead of half crazy.

'I just saw your ma a moment ago over in the healer's garden picking plants herself.' Pa's frown deepened and the grip on my shoulder got tighter. 'Are you spinning me stories, my girl? Are you up to mischief? 'Cause if you are on this night of all nights, then I swear I'll-'

He never got to finish, and I were right glad of that.

A sudden storm of howling and mooing and bleating and yelling went up from the south of the village like the fury of the four winds had broke upon our heads. Everyone dropped what they were doing and turned to stare in shock at the sight of the bulls and rams charging between the huts, knocking over everything in their path and running at each other with their great horns lowered.

'The animals have got loose!' came a shout. 'They're running amok!'

'Drive them back to the pens!' came another shout. 'Fence them in!'

'No that way! There's a lantern overturned in a hay bale and the blaze is causing a stampede!'

'Send them this way!'

'No, that way!'

'Ach, the pigs are loose and all!'

Pa let go of me and dashed away to help round up the stampeding cattle, and I couldn't help grinning at the chaos Bram had caused. Anyone who said my wee brother were useless just 'cause he were short one leg and had a shaky arm must be soft in the head. I didn't stop for long to admire his crafty work, though, but ran fast as I could to the brewing hut by the grain store. There were a row of cider barrels lined up by the fence, and after a quick look to make sure everyone were too busy chasing wayward sheep and cows to pay me any mind, I clambered up onto the nearest barrel and pulled myself over the fence posts. Ducking down on the other side so anyone looking out wouldn't see me, I crept towards the fields, keeping to the shadows and freezing any time I thought I saw the man at the gate looking my way.

But it weren't the eyes of the tribesfolk that were staring out at me. We didn't have mistletoe, but that didn't mean our Elders would let our village go undefended at Samhain. Tonight they'd had no choice but to make use of a magic even more ancient than the healer's herbs and the sacred plants of our ancestors. There were only one thing powerful enough to scare off the spirits of Samhain, and that were the souls of the dead. And that meant blood and sacrifice.

On top of each of the tallest fence posts, a skull glared out at me, dead eyes aglow with uncanny light from the bees-wax candles fixed inside. The flames guttered and flickered in the wind like the skulls were awake with malice and leering at the living. It were like a whole army of the dead were standing guard around our village. Bears and wildcats with their mouths open and their teeth bared, bulls and rams with their horns sharpened to wicked points, and stags with a great tangle of antlers as big as thorn bushes sat there watching me. Blood dripped down the fence in rivers so thick, they weren't yet dried in the fierce wind. I shivered with foreboding at the sight. If the Romans got their way, then it would be the skulls and the blood of my people painting our village white and red come tomorrow night.

There weren't no time to go brooding about that now, though. The full moon were giving me all the help it could by hiding behind the clouds, the frost were biting at my fingers and toes to keep me moving, and Felix were waiting for me down in the copse. Taking a deep breath, I turned away from the dead lights of the lanterns and went running off into the night.

Chapter Twenty

Felix

I thought she wasn't going to come.

Every moment that I waited seemed to last an hour, the mist curling up from the valley beyond Tintock Brae growing thicker as midnight approached. Frost spread like frozen cobwebs over the fallen leaves and the bare branches of the skeleton trees, turning the dead grass brittle under-foot. I could only hope the sentries on guard duty wouldn't hear our footsteps crunching all the way up to the wall.

'Come on, Jinny, where are you?' I muttered, blowing on my hands to heat my numb fingers. I had Jinny's tartan shawl tied tight around my shoulders, but it wasn't doing much to ward off the autumn chill. Winter was waiting right around the corner, and it was getting impatient. I knew how it felt. If Jinny didn't show up in the next few moments, I was going to have to go ahead without her. The best time for sneaking into the fort was between mid-night and the early hours of morning when the second night watch was getting sleepy and the fresher dawn watch hadn't yet taken over. If I missed this window, it would be too risky to try again later.

'I can't believe I agreed to do this,' I grumbled to the wind stirring the branches around the copse. 'What was I thinking?'

Was I really going to climb up the wall, creep past the guards, break into the barracks, and steal the eagle standard of the second Augustan legion right out from under their noses? What kind of a future would I have if I was caught? Would I end up a slave in a distant outpost of the empire, chained to the oars of a Roman ship, or fighting off lions in the Circus? None of those were the future I'd imagined or hoped for. I'd longed with all my heart to be a soldier like my father and fight for the glory of Rome. Even now, there was a part of me that wanted to abandon the whole crazy plan and go knocking on the fort gate begging for forgiveness. But if I did that, then innocent people would get killed tomorrow.

'I'm NOT a traitor,' I told myself for the hundredth time. 'Our Legate ordered us to keep the peace with the Damnonii until the Senate sends us south. I'm only trying to make sure those orders are carried out.'

But stealing the legion's standard? If Rome ever got to hear about it, then it would bring shame on the whole legion, including our Legate. I could only hope Brutus and the Senior Tribune would see sense, give back the Damnonii slaves, and buy peace in exchange for getting the standard back before anyone else got to hear about their eagle going missing.

'Wherever you are, Father,' I sighed, 'I'm so sorry about this. I wish you were here or that there was another way to solve this.'

'Talking to yourself, Roman boy?' a voice said in the darkness. 'Keep that up, and folks'll think the Samhain spirits have got into you.'

'Jinny! Finally! Have you brought the rope?'

Jinny stepped out from behind a tree and patted the pouch slung over her shoulder. 'Rope, knives, a sleeping draught pinched from our healer, and a big cloth to wrap the eagle in. I'm about as ready as I'll ever be. Here, take this.'

She handed me a sharp blade set in a bone handle, and I tucked it carefully into my belt. 'Thanks. Keep close to me – I know the path between the lilia pits, and you don't want to fall down on the spikes in the dark.'

'I don't want to be chased through the night by evil spirits neither, but since them metal men chose Samhain of all time to go stirring up trouble, I've no got much choice in the matter.'

'At least the stone giants turned out to be just a story,' I tried to smile to stop my teeth from chattering. 'They won't be coming for us, so that's one less thing to worry about.'

Jinny threw me an odd look and went strangely silent. I put it down to nerves, tightening my belt to keep the knife secure and hurrying out of the copse towards the wall.

For the first time, it seemed I was living up to my name, and luck was on my side. The moon was cloaked in cloud, and the sentries on top of the wall had lit lanterns to guide their way as they paced back and forth between the sentry towers. I could just make out the faint glow of light behind the wooden palisade, telling me exactly where each sentry stood. We wouldn't have much time to get over the wall between the guard posts before the pacing sentries reached us, so we'd have to be quick.

I crouched low as I crossed the wide strip of grass leading up to the wall, hoping the sentries wouldn't spot us in the darkness, or that if they did, they'd think we were just shadows thrown by the rolling clouds on the carpet of frost. I guided Jinny between the lilia pits, the dark patches of leaves and sticks marking the spots where the ground fell away in deep holes filled with spikes. We both knew now just how deadly those pits could be. I heard Jinny's breath catch in her throat as we tiptoed between the covered pits, and I reached back and squeezed her hand.

Don't think about the accident, I told her silently. *We've got work to do.*

Jinny seemed to hear me even though I didn't say a word, and she bit her lip, her eyes narrowing in concentration. She wanted to get this over with just as quickly as I did.

When we reached the wall, we flattened ourselves against the steep turf slope that led up to the wooden palisade at the top. The line of high fence posts cut into sharp spikes was a strong deterrent to wild animals and Damnonii warriors in heavy armour, but it wasn't much good against a desperate boy, a determined girl, and long piece of rope.

'See the soldier coming our way?' I whispered into Jinny's ear so the sound wouldn't carry. 'Once he's passed on to the next guard tower, we'll have only a couple of minutes to get over the fence before the next sentry comes this way. You ready?'

Jinny pulled the rope she'd brought from her leather pouch and nodded, keeping her eyes on the dim glow of light coming towards us through the cracks in the fence posts. The soft crunch of boots on gravel reached a crescendo as the guard drew level with the spot where we were hiding, then died away again as he passed on along the walkway. We waited until the night was silent once more, then sprang into action.

'Right, I'll give you a leg up. Be careful of those sharp posts,' I whispered, cupping my hands so Jinny could place her foot in the makeshift sling I made with my fingers. 'Ready? One, two, three!'

I heaved with all my might and Jinny went catapulting up to the top of the fence, grabbing for the spikes at the top and clinging on. Her feet scrabbled for grip against the stakes as she pulled herself over, then she clambered between the sharpened posts and disappeared behind the palisade. There was a soft thump of gravel on the other side, then silence again.

'Jinny? Jinny! Did you make it?' I whispered as loud as I dared. The end of a rope came sailing back over the fence in reply. I grabbed it, giving it a tug to make sure Jinny was holding fast to the other side, then began heaving myself up. The deep cut between my shoulder blades stung like I'd rolled in a patch of nettles as I climbed, but I gritted my teeth and kept going, hoping the pain would go away if I just ignored it for long enough. I'd only got halfway there when I heard the telltale crunch of boots approaching along the gravel walkway from the guard tower.

'Felix, shift your backside!' Jinny hissed from the other side of the fence. 'There's a soldier coming!'

I froze, one leg on the north side of the palisade, the other dangling down south. I couldn't make my mind up whether it was safer to jump back and wait for the guard to pass, or continue over to Jinny's side. Jinny made my mind up for me. She tugged sharply on the rope, pulling me off balance and sending me toppling over the fence to land in a heap at her feet. My back ached in protest, but for a long hopeful moment, I thought we'd got away with it. Then the approaching lantern light dipped and bobbed sharply as the sentry broke into a run.

'Quo vadis?' came a shout in the dark. 'Who goes there?'

'Quick!' I grabbed Jinny's hand and pulled her down the slope into the fort, ducking behind a huge pile of freshly sawn planks in the builders' yard.

'What's going on up there?'

Another set of boots came clomping around the barrack block, a group of soldiers led by an officer hurrying across the yard to the guard tower.

'Do you see something, soldier?' Brutus shouted again. 'Are the Damnonii attacking?'

'No, sir,' the guard called down, sounding a little sheepish. 'I thought I heard... It was just the wind, sir. Sorry.'

'You're not guarding the fort against falling leaves and figments of your imagination, soldier!' Brutus snorted. 'Get back to work. Keep your eyes peeled – those Damnonii will be attacking us any time now.'

'Yes, sir.' The lantern above us swung away towards the guard tower as the sentry hurried off.

'You three, check the Damnonii slaves in the prison block – make sure they're tied up securely,' Brutus told the soldiers in the yard. 'I don't want them making trouble from within when their tribe attacks the fort.'

'Yes, sir.' The soldiers marched off, and I waited to make sure the yard was empty before I let out a long breath.

'Phew! That was close! Right, we need to get inside the barrack block and look for the Standard Bearer with–' I stopped, feeling Jinny tense beside me. 'What is it? Do you hear something coming?'

'Felix, look!' Jinny wailed, stroking the pile of planks like it was made of precious metal and not just dead wood. 'Look what they've gone and done to our hallowed tree!'

'Jinny, I'm sorry...' It was feeble, but it was all I could say. There was no way to make up to Jinny what her tribe had lost. Hundreds of years of Damnonii history, tradition and culture were now sitting in a sawn-up heap, waiting to be turned into fence posts, roof beams and furniture for the Senior Tribune's dining room. It was no wonder the Damnonii were getting ready for war.

'Look, I know it hurts, but you have to try not to think about it right now, alright? We've got a job to do, and we don't have much time.'

Jinny tore her eyes from the piles of dead timber and swallowed down her anger. 'Where do we go now?' she asked through gritted teeth.

'The barrack block. It's the next group of buildings down from the officers' houses.'

'We likely to be seen?'

'Not if we're careful. Only the sentries should be up and about at this time.' I hoped Brutus was making sure the soldiers all got plenty of rest before the fight and that the gambling games behind the barrack block and cider drinking sessions by the cookhouse had wrapped up early.

We crept through the fort, keeping our backs pressed against the walls of each building we came to and ducking behind barrels and supply carts every time we heard the approaching boots of patrolling soldiers. The barrack block was dark and silent. The shutters were closed and a lone sentry stood in the doorway, stamping his feet to ward off the chill. My heart skipped a beat at the sight of him and his drawn sword. I'd been so focussed on sneaking over the wall into the fort, it hadn't occurred to me that getting into the soldiers' quarters might be the hard part.

'How we meant to get past him?' Jinny whispered. 'He don't look like he's going nowhere in a hurry.'

'Umm...'

I was casting about the dark street between the buildings, trying to come up with an idea that would move the guard from the doorway for long enough for us to get inside, when I caught sight of something that made my heart leap with hope.

'Look, Jinny, over there! It's the Standard Bearer!'

Septicus Strabo was sitting on the bathhouse steps, polishing the eagle standard with a cloth and talking in hushed tones with two centurions. A jug of cider stood on a barrel beside them, and for the first time that night, I really started to believe our plan might work after all.

'Jinny, did you say you stole a sleeping draught from your healer?' I whispered, trying to stop my voice squeaking with excitement.

'Aye, you thinking of dosing them metal men with it?' Jinny rummaged in her bag and pulled out a small clay pot with a thick wax stopper.

'Yes, if I can get close enough to that jug without them seeing me,' I said, taking the tiny pot and giving it a shake to see how much liquid was inside.

'Give it here, Roman boy, I'll do it. You got feet like a dancing bear, you have. You'll wake the whole camp with your stomping about.'

'Hey! That's not–'

'Ssh! If they catch me at it then you run like the wind and don't look back, got it? Don't stop till you're out of the fort and somewhere safe.'

I didn't see much point in reminding her that with a

war being planned for dawn, there wasn't a single safe place left anymore. I just gulped and nodded.

Jinny took the little clay pot and crept round the side of the barrack block, her shadow blending into the dark shapes the soldiers' lanterns cast along the street between the buildings. I held my breath the whole time it took her to reach the barrel where the cider jug stood, and I'd almost suffocated when she finally crouched down behind it, hidden from sight.

One of the centurions glanced round with a slight frown as though he heard something, but Strabo hit him on the arm to turn his attention back to the joke he was telling, and he looked away again. I couldn't hear the low voices of the three men, but I knew from Strabo's eager polishing and the way the second centurion was stroking the blade of his sword that they were talking about the coming war and what they were going to do to the Damnonii when the fort was attacked. When I saw the grin on the Standard Bearer's face at the thought of the killing to come, any guilt I felt at the trouble he'd be in when the legion's eagle went missing on his watch vanished into thin air.

Strabo reached out for the cider jug suddenly, and I had to bite back a yell when his hand nearly collided with Jinny's. She snatched hers back behind the barrel again, and I could only watch and hope she'd managed to get the sleeping draught inside before Strabo filled the three cups. The joking and muffled laughter continued as the men drank, and I was almost ready to give up and admit defeat when the first centurion's knees buckled and he pitched forward onto the steps. Then the second centurion staggered, dropping his cup and sinking slowly to the ground.

Strabo stared at them opened-mouthed for a moment, then his own amazement turned into a yawn that ended in a loud snore.

I waited, tense with excitement, until Jinny's head popped back up above the barrel and she waved me over. 'They're out cold. Quick! Grab that big pole and hide it in this so it don't go glinting in the lantern light and giving us away,' Jinny whispered, pulling a length of sackcloth from her bag.

I wrapped the eagle standard carefully, my hands trembling at the thought of being caught in the act of treason. 'We're giving this straight back in exchange for the prisoners, right, Jinny?' I asked for what must have been the thousandth time. 'Your Elders wouldn't be stupid enough to try to keep it in revenge for the tree, would they?'

'We can't give it back afore we've even took it in the first place,' Jinny hissed. 'Now move your backside, Roman boy – we need to get out of here!'

I wasn't much reassured by her answer, but I couldn't argue. The sound of footsteps was approaching, and it wouldn't be long before the sentries doing the rounds of the camp found the three men out cold on the bathhouse steps.

We tiptoed back round the barrack block and officers' houses, choosing a different stretch of wall to make our escape this time. That guard who'd nearly run into us would have his eyes skinned for shadows in the dark now that Brutus had given him a dressing down. We were just about to step round the corner of the kitchens, when a group of four figures detached themselves from the wall of the prison block and came marching towards us. The first figure held a lantern, and in its flickering light I saw Capito grinning smugly, a sharp knife in his hand.

For one horrible moment, I thought we'd been seen. My own hand reached for the bone-handled blade I'd tucked into my belt, pulling it out and readying for a fight.

Then, instead of rushing up to grab us, Capito and his gang stopped by the storehouse door, laughing and whispering like they were cooking up some nasty little plot. The three other boys watched as Capito bent down, fitting the blade of his knife into the heavy padlock chained to the door.

'You sure you can spring the lock?' one of the boys asked doubtfully.

'No bother. I'll have those meat pies and sugared plums out before you can count to twenty.'

As usual, Capito was making an empty boast. It took him a lot longer than that.

By the time he finally got the padlock off, I could hear the footsteps of the sentries marching up the street behind us. We were going to be caught between two groups of Romans, and there was no way for us to get out without being seen.

'We have to make a run for it, Jinny!' I whispered. 'If we can get back over the wall maybe the guards won't catch us.'

'Don't be a deadwit!' Jinny hissed back. 'Them metal men won't let us loose once they've got our scent, and their swords and arrows are no going to miss in the dark, no even if they've got their eyes shut.'

'But the soldiers are coming!'

'Don't pee yourself, Roman boy – I got an idea.'

Jinny bent down, grabbing a handful of stones and pulling her sling from her pocket. I didn't see how one leather catapult was going to be much use against a soldier in full armour. But then I realised she wasn't aiming for the sentries coming down the street behind us, she was aiming for the group of boys crowding round the storehouse door.

With a soft whoosh of air, a stone went whizzing towards them, smacking Capito hard on the backside as he leaned down over the lock. He leapt up with a yelp of pain, rounding on the boy standing behind him.

'What was that for, Pansa, huh? You think that's funny?'

'What?' The other boy scowled, stepping back and balling his fists. 'What are you talking about?'

Another stone whooshed through the air, striking one of the boys on the side of the head. He spun round and shoved Capito hard in the chest. 'What's wrong with you, Capito? You lost your nerve or something? Looking for a fight so you don't have to go through with the storehouse dare?'

'Shut your mouth, Lupus. You're the coward, not me.'

'I'm not the one who's worried Daddy's going to catch me and beat me with his belt!'

'I'm not scared of my father!' Capito yelled, shoving the boy right back.

All it took was another couple of well-aimed stones to set the flaring tempers on fire. A moment later, the four boys were rolling on the ground, pummelling each other with their fists and snarling like a pack of dogs. Just as the sentries coming down the street got close enough to make us out by the light of the lanterns, we bolted past the group of fighting boys and made a dash for the slope of the wall.

We heard yelling coming from behind us, but when I looked back, the sentries were grabbing Capito and his friends round the neck and hauling them to their feet, demanding to know what was going on. We hadn't been seen. I grabbed Jinny's arm and raced up to the walkway, barely stopping for breath till we were over the palisade and running for the cover of the copse once more.

When we reached the screen of trees and looked back to see there was nothing chasing us through the dark, I thought we'd managed to escape and were out of danger.

I was wrong.

Chapter Twenty One

Jinny

I wanted to hang around and watch the fight. There weren't nothing I liked better than seeing one nasty wee Roman knocking lumps out of another one, but Felix were mad keen to get back over the wall, so I missed all the best bits.

I were that out of breath with the jitters and running by the time we made it back to the copse that I couldn't speak for half an age. Instead I just bent over my knees and sucked in great gulps of air, feeling the frost sting the back of my throat and the thick mist near strangle the life out of me. Felix crouched down and cradled that golden bird on its pole like it were a baby wrapped in nursing cloths, muttering that he were a traitor to Rome and his pa would kill him if he ever found out. Seeing it were clear as ice that his pa were dead and gone, I didn't see how that were going to happen. Still, I let him be for a bit, hoping my own pa were still busy with the cattle round-up and no raging at me for having run off.

In the dead of night, the fog rising up from the Luggie smothered the world in a damp blanket so heavy, it were hard to see more than a few paces ahead. All the sounds of the night creatures were timid and faint, like they were afeared of choking on the mist. It were eerie, that emptiness, and I wanted nothing more than to get the job finished and get back to my own safe bedroll as fast as I could.

'Come on, Felix, them Romans'll raise the alarm any minute now. We should get ourselves far away as we're able to afore they come looking for their bird.'

Felix nodded and pulled himself back up like he had the weight of the whole world sitting on his shoulders instead of just a big pole with an eagle on top. We clambered up the slope to the meadow, our feet crunching and sliding on the thick frost covering the grass. We'd agreed to dig a hole in the corner of the turnip field under the hawthorn bushes and hide the metal pole there for the time being, as the farmers wouldn't be touching the soil with their hoes again till spring. But the ground were that hard with cold, I were starting to think twice about the plan. I hadn't thought to leave out a spade, and we'd scrape our hands raw if we tried digging a hidey-hole without one.

'Do you think we should maybe find another spot to leave the bird in for now?' I asked as we cleared the slope and began trudging our way through the mist in the meadow. 'I can't see us digging a deep enough hole in the field without a tool to work with, and my hands are chilled to the bone with cold already. Maybe we should –'

I stopped, a sudden sound in the night sending shivers down my spine.

'Did you hear that?' I grabbed Felix by the wrist and pulled him to a stop.

'What?' he whispered, his breath coming out in nervous puffs of steam. 'What did you hear? Is it the Romans?'

The sound came again, and this time he heard it too. I felt his arm go stiff like he were turned to ice on the spot. A low whistling were rising and falling on the wind, following us through the mist and closing in as we stood there shivering in the dark.

'It's them!' I gasped. 'The stone giants are awake and

walking the night!'

'I don't see anything.' Felix strained his eyes till they were just wee narrow slits, then shook his head, looking back at me like I were crazy. 'Jinny, you had me scared for a minute. That sound's just the wind howling through the trees.'

'It's the stone giants whistling the ancient song!' I insisted, 'and it's no the first time I've heard them at it! They're awake and coming for me, Felix, they're still angry at me for waking them! I've seen them afore, walking through the fields to the village.'

'What? But it's just a story!' Felix shook his head, no wanting to believe a word I said. 'Look, after that day in the circle, I thought I'd been seeing them too in the mist, but it was all just my imagination. And even if it's not, you said you put mistletoe round the circle to send them to sleep! How can they have left the valley?'

I didn't know how to answer that, but I didn't need to. The proof were right before my very eyes. There were a great shadow moving in the mist, shifting just beyond my line of sight. Every time I fixed my gaze on it, the dark shape stopped, melting back into the fog. The whistling died away, only to start up again as soon as I took a step forward, like it were following close on our heels.

'See?' I hissed, pointing into the mist. 'It's right over there!'

'I still can't see anything. Maybe it's just the remains of the hallowed tree that looks like a standing stone in the dark,' Felix whispered, peering into the night. 'It's probably the fog swirling round it and making you think it's moving. It fooled me that day in the circle too.'

'The stump them metal men left is no taller than my kneecaps!' I snapped, shuddering when the shape reappeared again so close I could smell the damp and moss on the ancient rock. 'We've no got time to argue about it, Felix! Run!'

I grabbed the edge of the shawl he were wearing and took off across the meadow, no much caring if I strangled him, so long as we both escaped. The whistling were growing so loud it were almost a shriek; another shadow, then another flickered behind the curtain of mist. One minute the shapes were behind us, the next they were running at our side. Then before I knew it, there were a huge stone towering before us, and I went tumbling to the ground in a heap, pulling Felix down with me. I rolled onto my knees, shaking with terror as the giants slid out of the mist and circled around us.

'Felix, get up!' I yelled. 'We got to move or they'll kill us!'

'Jinny... I can't run any further... my shoulder... hurts.' Felix were panting and his face were so pale I thought he were going to pass out. He'd been hiding how much his shoulder were grieving him all night, but now there were spots of blood coming through the shawl and I knew he'd torn it open again with the effort to keep up with me. I couldn't leave him behind, but I couldn't outrun the stones in the dark with him holding me back. We weren't neither of us going to escape this.

I gritted my teeth and summoned up every last bit of courage I had, forcing myself to look up at the stone giant standing over us. 'What do you want?' I yelled, my voice shaking so hard I couldn't hardly get the words out. 'Why can you no just go back to sleep and let us be?'

The stone giant just stood there, like it were waiting. The others were watching us further back in the fog, and I couldn't see no more of them than the black outline of rock through the dark. But this one were so close, I could see the chunk of stone I'd smashed out of its head, the dark patch on the other side looking so like an eye glaring out at me from the mist I near peed myself with terror. For a long moment, we just stared at each other without moving. Then the stone giant lurched forward.

I let out a shriek that must've been heard all the way to the wall.

But the stone weren't coming for me. It walked straight past, gliding back into the mist with the other shapes. I held my breath, clenching my hands into fists so tight, I couldn't hardly feel the blood in my fingers. Then the whistling started up again behind us. First it moved away through the mist, then it echoed back like it were calling to me, the dark shape hovering just out of sight like it were waiting for something.

'Jinny, what are you doing?' Felix demanded. 'You're acting crazy!'

'Did you no see it?' I gasped. 'Felix, it were right on top of us!'

'You're seeing things,' he muttered, clutching his shoulder like it were ready to fall off with the pain. 'And even if they were chasing us like you think, why would the stones just go away again without attacking us?'

'I don't know,' I stammered, my mind a whirl of strange thoughts. 'I think maybe...'

'What?'

'Felix, I think they want us to follow them.'

'WHAT?' This time Felix yelled the word like I were deaf as well as crazy. 'You can't be serious! We have to get out of here before the Romans come looking for us! I'm too tired and too sore to go chasing shadows in the night.'

But the more I heard the uncanny sound of whistling in the dark, and the more I looked at them stones slipping in and out of the mist, the more sure I got that they weren't coming to kill us. No, that weren't it at all. They were trying to lead us somewhere.

'Come on, there's something they want us to see.'

'You're out of your mind.' Felix weren't none too happy, but he also weren't none too steady on his feet neither, so he didn't have no choice but to drape his arm round my shoulder and let me support him as we went wherever I chose to go.

And I chose to follow the stones.

Through the mist they led us, keeping close as they shepherded us across the meadow and up onto the sheiling. The vast pastureland were empty and shivering in the autumn chill, the wind howling over the frost-caked grass and shaking the thin branches of the trees. The mist were thinner up here, the shadows of the walking stones blending into the jet black of the sky until it were hard to make out if I were following something real or just the fevered ghosts of my imagination. The only thing clear in my head were the whistling, the uncanny sound rising and falling on the wind just out of reach, drawing us on across the pastures.

'Jinny, I can't keep going much longer,' Felix panted at last, sinking down to sit on one knee. 'You go. I'll wait here and rest.' He set the heavy bundle of the wrapped-up pole down and tried to rub the feeling back into his stiff neck.

'Just a wee bit further, Felix... See! They've stopped over there.' I pointed to the ditch where the stones stood in a row, facing us in the dark.

'Where? I still don't see them.'

'Are you blind?' I could've hit him for being so dead-witted, but he were hurting bad enough already. 'Look, they're... Oh.'

When I turned back, the stones had gone.

I stood still and listened hard. The only sounds I heard in the darkness were the whoosh of the wind in the grass and the hooting of a night owl in the distance. The whistling had died away as sudden as it started, leaving me standing in the cold without half a clue what I were doing there.

'Hello?' I called, feeling like the biggest fool who ever walked the earth. 'Is there anybody there?'

Nothing. The night were no more haunted with the spirits of stone giants than the Luggie were full of kelpies. I'd been following the willow-the-wisps of my imagination through the dark, nothing more.

'I'm such a feather-brain!' I muttered. 'I could've sworn I heard–'

All of a sudden, Felix clutched my arm so tight, I thought he were going to pull it off.

'Ow! Let go, you daftie! What's got into you?'

'Ssh!' Felix said, his face glowing with excitement. 'Listen!'

I strained my ears, but there weren't nothing in the night save that the wailing wind and the cursed owl that wouldn't shut up. 'There ain't nothing out there, Felix. Let's go.'

But Felix weren't going nowhere with me. No yet. He closed his eyes and listened again, then he went stumbling off across the pasture to the ditch where I'd last seen sight of the stones.

'Hey! Where you going?'

Seeing as I'd just dragged him halfways to the Camsith Fells, I couldn't hardly complain about following him across a wee field, so I hurried to catch up, grabbing him and holding him steady so he wouldn't go toppling head-first into the ditch in his eagerness. When I looked down and saw what were in there, I near swallowed my own tongue with surprise.

There were a man in the ditch – a Roman with a scuffed leather undershirt and dents all across his breastplate. But it weren't his armour needing polished that were the worst of his troubles. A mess of blood had seeped out of the wounds in his side, caking his breastplate like rust and staining his tunic almost black. He must've been walking for many sundowns after he got them cuts, as I could see strips of darkened cloth peeking out from under his shirt where he'd tied himself up to stop the bleeding. His brown skin were slick with the sweat of fever, and it were only the wee wisps of breath turning to steam in the cold night air that showed us he were still alive.

Felix sank to his knees, half dead with amazement. 'Father!' he cried, 'it's me, Felix!' Then he said a whole string of Latin words that I didn't catch, but the metal man must have, 'cause he shivered and opened his eyes. I knew right then and there he were definitely Felix's pa. His eyes were the exact shade of dark brown, his cropped hair screwing up into the same wee curls close to his head. He blinked slowly a couple of times like he couldn't hardly believe what he were seeing, then he gave a weak smile and patted Felix on the cheek, gasping out a few words of Latin and struggling to sit up.

We helped move him out of the ditch, but he were that tired and weak he couldn't stay standing for more than a few moments, even though Felix and me tried to hold him up between us. When he'd sank back down again for the third time I said, 'This is no good, Felix. You stay here with your pa and I'll run back to the village and fetch help.'

'He's badly wounded,' Felix shook his head. 'I don't know if he'll last that long out here in the cold.'

'We've no got much choice, have we? I'll go as fast as I can.'

'But what if they won't come and help?' Felix said, his face all screwed up with worry. 'The Damnonii are about to go to war with the Romans – what if they just kill him instead?'

'What else can you and me do? We can't bring him to the fort in the dead of night,' I told him. 'You saw them archers up on the wall ready to fire down on anyone walking up to the gate. We'll have to take him somewhere safe till daybreak, and the closest place is our village. Give me the metal bird so I can show them our tribe's got the upper hand and I'll try to make them see sense.'

I could see Felix were none too happy about parting with the one bargaining chip he had left with the Damnonii. But he handed it over anyway, and it warmed my heart to see that as well as fear over what might happen, there were trust for me in his eyes too.

'Alright, Jinny. Please hurry.'

I nodded and turned back to race down the sheiling and across the fields to Waterside.

That were when I heard the whistling again.

This time, it were a sharp piercing sound that cut the air and sent the birds that were roosting in the bushes flapping away for higher ground.

I'd never been so glad to hear such an awful din in all my life.

I stuck my fingers in my mouth and whistled back with all my might like my life depended on it. A few moments later the whistle came again, closer this time. Then I saw something that made my heart leap with joy.

Bram were cantering across the sheiling, heading our way like he had the four winds of winter at his back. 'Jinny!' he called. 'Jinny, are you alright?'

'Aye, Bram! And right glad to see you, though I should be mad you're no doing what you were told and staying put at home. What in the name of the wee fairy folk are you doing out for a ride on a night like this?'

'I heard you whistling for me, Jinny,' Bram panted, pulling Tramper up short and gaping at the Roman man stretched out on the grass. 'I heard you whistling that old song Grandma taught you.'

'What are you babbling about?' I frowned. 'I weren't whistling! I were too busy running for my life from one end of the night to the other.'

'But it were you, Jinny, I swear! No one whistles as bad and as out of tune as you, I'd know that sound anywhere!'

Bram and me stared at each other for a long moment,

trying to puzzle it out, but then Felix reminded us what the most important problem to solve were. 'Bram, my father's hurt badly. Can we use your pony to get him back to the village?'

'Your pa?' Bram looked at the man in amazement. 'He's no dead then?'

'He will be if he doesn't get help soon.'

Lucky for us, Bram were never one to ask a string of questions when there were a job to be done. Soon Felix and his pa were sitting up on Tramper, and I were giving my wee brother a piggyback across the sheiling. I looked back every now and then when we reached the fields, but the mist had drifted away to the valley and the night were still and silent. Even the wind had died, and the skull lanterns glowing in the distance looked warm and friendly as they welcomed us back home.

I crossed my fingers in the dark, praying to the four winds that the greeting me and Bram were going to get would be friendly too. It weren't likely, what with us bringing a Roman boy and a soldier back to our village on the eve of war. I could only hope that once the Elders saw the eagle and heard our plan for peace, they'd agree to protect Felix and his pa. If they didn't, then I were leading them like lambs to the slaughter block.

I'll stick my neck under the axe afore I let them hurt a boy who's done so much to keep them safe, I vowed, screwing up my courage and marching right up to the gate. *Just you wait and see if I don't. This time, I'll no let the Elders push me around like I'm a wee lassie. I'm the one who's going to stop this war, whether the Council likes it or no.*

Chapter Twenty Two

Felix

The healer took so long over my father, I thought he'd passed away and she was putting off telling me till I got some rest. But when she finished tying the bandages and got up from the bed, there was a faint smile on her face and her eyes were hopeful.

'I've done the best I can. You need to let him sleep for now,' she told me.

'But you think he'll be alright?' I asked, not quite believing anyone so still could be anywhere but the brink of death.

'With a bit of luck, he'll be fine.' The healer smiled, and the relief flooded through me so fast I thought I was going to pass out. My father always said I was all the luck he ever needed, so maybe if I just stayed by his side, I could pull him through this with me.

'Here, I'll change that dressing on your back for you. Jinny may have a good heart, but she's as much use with a bandage and a poultice as a sheep is with a set of knitting needles.' The healer set about washing the deep cut between my shoulder blades, covering my back with a thick paste that smelled of mint and stung a lot less than the one Jinny had used.

'Do you know what happened to my father?' I asked, eying the arrowhead the healer had pulled from my father's side. It had a wicked barb that had to be cut out with a knife, but it had plugged the worst of my father's wounds and kept him from bleeding out as he struggled to get home.

'That's a Maeatae arrowhead. They probably caught your pa's band of soldiers as they were crossing the Camsith Fells. He were right fortunate – they're no usually sloppy enough to leave a man alive once the warriors have got the scent of blood in their nostrils.'

'He must have walked for days with that arrow in his side trying to get back!' I shuddered.

'Aye, he's a brave one. Here, I found this in his tunic.' She handed me a piece of tanned leather that had a map carved into it showing the mountains, rivers and coastlines of the north all the way up to a broad headland at the very tip of the great island. I grinned when I saw it. I'd have to show Bram the world didn't just drop away in a big hole after all.

'He did it!' I smiled, proud and amazed at the same time. 'He mapped the whole of the wild north!'

'Hmph, well I don't know if I can let you hang onto that,' the healer frowned, all the lines on her face crinkling up till she looked like a wizened grape. 'The last thing we need is more metal men marching over our land building walls everywhere and killing our tribesfolk.'

'You don't need to worry about the army,' I said, tucking the leather map into my belt before she could confiscate it. 'They'll be marching south any day now, and I doubt you'll hear from them again for a couple of lifetimes at least.'

'What makes you say that?'

'The Romans are leaving. They're being ordered back to Hadrian's Wall in the south.'

'The Council will be right glad to hear that,' Jinny's father said, stepping into the healer's hut without knocking at the door. He looked like he was in too much of a hurry for politeness, and I shrank back at the grim look on his face as he eyed me and my father. 'Put your shirt on, lad, and come with me,' he ordered. 'The Council want to hear your side of the story before we make a decision.'

I gulped and pulled on my shirt as fast as I could, hiding the map under it so he wouldn't ask what it was. I followed him out of the hut and through the village, feeling the eyes of every Damnonii in the land drilling into my head as we crossed the main square where the blacksmith was hard at work at his anvil. He was busy hammering sword and axe blades into shape, and groups of warriors were gathered round whetstones and grinding blocks, sharpening their weapons into vicious points. The Council clearly hadn't given any orders to stop the war preparations.

The sky was turning pink and gold in the east, the dawn breaking after a long night. Soon the Damnonii from every village from here to the Camsith Fells would be marching out of Waterside to storm the steep slopes of the Antonine Wall, and most would never make it home. The Roman fort was too well defended, their archers too accurate and their armour too strong. No one ever beat the Romans in a straight fight. It just wasn't a fair contest.

Maybe there's still time to talk the Council into making peace, I thought. *Maybe it's not too late to get them to agree to a trade.*

But when I stepped into the huge round Council hut and saw the red-hot fury on Jinny's face as she stood glaring at the assembled Elders, I knew the battle had already begun, and we weren't winning. Bram was sitting on a bench beside her, biting his lip in frustration. The eagle standard of the second Augustan legion lay glittering in the candlelight on the floor before the Elders. They were frowning at it and whispering to each other, clearly not convinced that the loss of something even so awe-inspiring could bring a whole Roman legion to its knees. *They can just make another one,* I heard them mutter. *Not like our hallowed tree.*

Gregor was propped up in a chair with a pile of blankets and cushions, and although his eyes were half closed, I could tell he was listening intently. The village chief might be badly injured, but at least he was paying attention.

'That's no what I were saying at all!' Jinny was yelling, looking ready to launch herself at the Elders and shake some sense into them. 'I never said nothing about sneaking into the fort to free the slaves, it were to get the golden bird and bring it here.'

'So you're telling us you were inside Caerpen Taloch, knowing full well my Connor and the two other lads and lassie were locked up there, and you never thought to get them out and bring them home instead of this shiny wee bauble that ain't no use to no one?' Ailsa looked like she was ready to pick the eagle standard up and clobber Jinny over the head with it to knock some sense into her. Jinny wisely took three steps back and did her glowering from there.

'The eagle's not just some fancy ornament!' I jumped straight in to help Jinny out. 'It's the symbol of the whole legion – they won't go to war without it. Men will die defending it, and when they find that it's missing, they'll do anything to get it back.'

'You mean they'll slaughter every man, woman and bairn in our whole tribe to find it?' Jinny's father snapped. 'Then what in the four winds were the three of you thinking bringing it here? You've taken all the surprise out of our attack – them Romans'll be arming for war now you've given them a good reason for one.'

'What we've done is give them a good reason to *avoid* war,' I said. 'Just listen.' I took a deep breath, explaining all about the Senate's coming orders for the legions at the Antonine Wall to draw back south, our Legate's strict instruction not to start a war with the tribe, our Senior Tribune's plot with Brutus to stir up trouble to keep the legion posted at Caerpen Taloch, and the lengths they'd go to hide the loss of the eagle standard to protect their status.

'So you see,' I panted, almost out of breath, 'if we can make a deal with Taurus, the Senior Tribune, to return the legion's standard in exchange for releasing the slaves and not causing any more trouble, then we can avoid a war altogether and no one else needs to get hurt!'

'But what about our hallowed tree?' Morag, the senior Elder, asked, frowning at me like I'd forgotten the most important point of all. 'What about the tribesfolk the metal men killed in cold blood the other day? Are we just to let all that go unavenged?'

I wasn't sure how to answer that. It was Jinny who spoke up, surprising us all with her answer. 'Revenge is for bairns who don't know no better,' she said. 'If we start another war with the Romans now, just when they're about to leave anyhow, then when's the killing and avenging ever going to stop? Instead of peace for the next lot of bairns to come, we'll just be piling up grief in their winter grain store, and they'll no thank us for that. We got a chance to end the troubles once and for all, and we should be grabbing it with both hands.'

There was silence for a long moment, everyone looking at Jinny in amazement. 'See, Jin?' Bram grinned. 'I told you that you had a good head on your shoulders if you'd just cool your temper and bother to use your brain once in a while.'

'It were you and Felix who taught me forgiveness, Bram, and I've taken a long time learning the lesson. It's no been an easy one, but I think I'm getting the hang of it.'

She looked up to see her father beaming at her, and she blushed bright red at the sudden attention. Morag and the other Elders muttered together for a bit longer, then they reached an agreement.

'You've run a right risk, the three of you,' she said. 'And I'm no saying we're no still mad about the liberties you've taken when a war were at stake, but you may just have given us the best chance of peace we're likely to get.'

The other Elders nodded, but Gregor sat up straighter in his chair, beckoning me closer and looking me straight in the eye like he was sizing me up. 'You've proved you don't mean us no harm despite your Roman blood, and I suppose we've got your mother to thank for that,' he wheezed like the words were an effort. 'But as to talking the soldiers at Caerpen Taloch into releasing the slaves and leaving us be in exchange for this golden bird, that's another thing entirely. How do we know the metal men will even listen to a wee spit of a lad like you who's already shown them he's no exactly sure which side of the wall he prefers sitting on?' Gregor gave me a stern look, and the Elders all stared at me expectantly, waiting for an answer.

I gulped. It was a fair point. I had no idea how I was going to talk Taurus into accepting the deal. I wasn't even sure they'd let me get within half a mile of the front gate without the archers shooting me in the head.

'They won't listen to the boy,' a voice said from the doorway. 'But they will listen to me.' The words were halting and heavily accented, like the speaker was struggling with a foreign tongue he'd learned a long time ago but hadn't used since. I'd know that voice anywhere. My mother used to laugh at him and the way he strangled the vowels, but I knew she appreciated the effort he made to talk to her in her own language.

We all turned to the door. My father was standing there, clutching the bandages at his side and breathing heavily. He looked at the Council, down at the eagle standard on the floor, then over to me. I waited, holding my breath for a long, anxious moment. Was he going to be angry at me for bringing shame on the second Augustan legion? Was he going to understand why I'd done something so desperate to save the Damnonii? Or was he going to think I was a traitor to Rome?

That moment seemed to last a lifetime. My father didn't frown, but he didn't smile either. All he did was give a small nod of approval, and all the long months of loneliness and worry vanished like smoke on the wind.

'Well done, Felix,' he said in Latin. 'You've done your best to make sure our Legate's orders are carried out and the peace treaty holds. I'm proud of you, my boy.'

I couldn't be sure, but I think I might have blushed just as red as Jinny's hair at that.

Chapter Twenty Three

Jinny

There weren't going to be no war after all.

I were right glad of that, but truth be told, I weren't exactly jumping for joy at the thought of Felix going back to the fort again and leaving for good with the soldiers. I were happy that he'd got his pa back in near enough one piece, and that I'd got over the urge to knock his head off with any rock that were close to hand, but still...

My wee brother weren't mad keen on Felix leaving neither, but as we all trooped up to the wall for the exchange, Bram were too busy asking him questions about where the soldiers were going next to have time to look sad at the parting.

The new peace treaty were all fixed up: Felix's pa had been to the wall to talk to the man called Taurus and got him to agree to the exchange. I wished I got to see that Roman chief's face when he found out their bird had been pinched right out from under their noses, but I weren't allowed to go along to the meeting. We Damnonii hung back, just in case the peace talks broke down and the Romans decided they'd just march out and take their bird back at sword point. But it turned out, the Roman chief were so worried about the rest of the soldiers finding out about the eagle going missing and him losing his position, that he were ready to agree to just about anything to hush it up.

That weren't all that were kept quiet. It were a fair bet Felix's pa didn't mention nothing about Felix being the one to sneak in and steal the bird, so at least they'd got no reason to stop him returning to the fort and joining their army when he were good and ready. Felix were so happy about that, I didn't have the heart to ask him why he wanted to join up with a bunch of soldiers who went around thieving other folks' land and taking them all as slaves, especially as he were half Damnonii and could've stayed with us instead. But his pa were a Roman officer and Felix looked up to him, so I reckoned it were only natural for him to want to be just like him. I figured we all want to stick with what we know best in the end. Maybe Felix learned enough from his time here that he'd be a better Roman soldier than the ones at Caerpen Taloch, and he'd no take slaves nor steal from folk when he were in charge of things.

Maybe.

Either way, he were leaving and that thought had me dragging my heels worse than Tramper when she were in a right huff.

'Jinny, what's up with you?' Bram asked, seeing my face all screwed up with the grumps. 'Are you no happy we're getting the slaves back and the Romans are leaving without a war?'

'Aye, of course, Bram,' I sighed. 'It's just...'

'What?' He nudged Tramper up beside me, and I gave her a pat to stop her chewing my hair as we walked. There were that many folks come out to see the exchange, it looked half like the war were going ahead after all. I were pretty sure they were all a wee bit worried the Romans wouldn't keep their word and would just take their golden bird back and send their soldiers out to meet us. The Damnonii were all here to make a show of force to put them off the idea.

But Felix's pa were sure the deal would go ahead, and he had a kind of quiet confidence that made folk trust him even though he were a Roman and spoke our language like he were chewing a mouthful of nettles. It were funny, but I'd only just noticed that Felix were the dead spit of him, and no just in looks. He'd got me to trust him despite being so mad I'd wanted to knock his head off, and that were no easy thing to do.

'What is it, Jinny?' Felix asked. 'Are you worried the Romans won't keep their word?'

'No, you pair of dafties, I'm no worried about nothing!' I sighed. 'It just... I don't like the way everything's changing, that's all.'

'You don't want the metal men to leave and give us our land back?' Bram looked at me like I were soft in the head.

'Course I do! But do you have to go with them, Felix? You could stay here and live in our village – we can always do with extra hands at planting time, and the herders would no complain about having another lad to train up. Your pa could probably stay too – he speaks enough of our language to get by, and the tribe won't look too badly on him seeing as your ma were a Damnonii woman.'

Felix shook his head, and I could see he were sad at the thought of leaving too. 'I grew up here, but it's not where I belong, not really,' he said.

'But you're half Damnonii!' I said. 'Don't that make this land your home?'

Felix shrugged and looked away for a bit till he were sure he weren't going to cry. It were an odd thing to admit, but I looked on him all the better for being half torn at the thought of going away. 'Maybe one day, when I've seen more of the world, I'll think of this as home and come back to stay for good,' he said. 'But right now, there's so much to see, so many places to go, that I can't make my mind up where I belong. My father's got a few years left till he can retire from the army, so once we've spent some time at Hadrian's Wall, we'll go to Rome, and then I'll be old enough to join the army and go on adventures of my own.'

'Adventures!' Bram sighed like it were the most glorious word in the world. 'That sounds thrilling! I wish I could come with you, Felix.'

'What, and go stomping all over other tribes' land and stealing away slaves?' I snorted. 'You're a Damnonii, Bram, and that's no what our folk do. Leave it to the Romans. Anyhow, what d'you want to see the world for when you've got the prettiest spot on earth to live in with four seasons of change every year to look forward to?'

I pointed out across our land as we crossed the high strip of grass leading up to the wall. Behind us the Camsith Fells were glowing green and gold against the bright blue sky, and the birds were dancing overhead as they made their way south for the winter. It were a cold day, the air so crisp I could taste the tang of coming winter with each breath I took. The fairies had been busy hanging their frost on the trees and grass early in the morning, but now that the sun were up, it had all turned into balls of dew that glittered from each branch and blade of grass like starlight.

'You'll have adventures of your own, Bram, I promise you that,' Felix smiled, slipping him a piece of leather with a bunch of markings carved on it. 'I made a copy of my father's map. Maybe one day you can go north and find out for yourself if the world really does end in a giant hole that sucks all the water down. And once the Romans have gone, there'll be nothing stopping you going south either. You could even come and visit me at Hadrian's Wall!'

My heart leapt at the thought of the wall coming down and opening up a path to the southern horizon. I'd always wondered where the birds that flew south for the winter went and what they saw there. Maybe now I'd have a chance to find out for myself one day.

'Sheesh, thanks Felix!' Bram grinned, tucking the map into his tunic like it were a rare piece of treasure. 'What do you think, Jin? If the harvest next year does well, maybe we can talk Pa into getting you a horse too, and we could ride off adventuring!'

'Thanks, Bram,' I laughed. 'But I think a big hunting dog would suit me better than a daft wee pony, especially against them wild tribes Felix's pa came up against.'

'What about a dog then?' Bram looked at me sideways like he were trying out an idea he'd been sitting on for a while. 'Gregor's black hound is ready for pups now, and I know he'd give you one if you asked him nice. You might even get lucky and get another runt to turn into a fine big beast like Raggy.'

I bit my lip. No one had brought up dogs around me since my Raggy died, knowing I'd bite their head off as soon as they opened their mouth. It still hurt to think of him, but the sting weren't as sharp as it once were, and now the thought of another wee pup sitting in the basket I still kept by my bedroll didn't seem like such a terrible betrayal after all.

'Maybe, Bram,' I smiled back. 'We'll see.'

'Alright, that's far enough!' A shout came from the front

of the group, and all of us Damnonii stopped on the grass a good two field lengths from the big gate in the wall. We might trust Felix's pa to make the deal without trouble, but we weren't daft enough to give the Romans a close enough target to tempt their archers.

Felix's pa went up to the gate and knocked, and a moment later it opened with a loud creak and a bunch of soldiers marched out to stand on the wee bridge. Then a big man who looked like he'd had too many roast dinners came clomping out, followed by two metal men I'd know from even ten times the distance. They were the two who were in the copse that day when Bram and me were hunting rabbits. I couldn't be sure from where I stood, but I thought they were looking all nervous and shifty like they were so wound up with worrying they needed to pee for a week to get rid of the jitters. It made me smile to myself to think on them being turned so meek after all their blustering and bullying.

Ailsa and Pa walked up to meet them, carrying the standard wrapped up in cloth. There was so much of the stuff bundled round it, you wouldn't know if it were a plank of wood, a gift of tartan blankets or a hunk of meat all wrapped up to the keep the flies off it. The big man standing at the gate must've told Felix's pa to cover the eagle up so the soldiers wouldn't know their bird had been pinched. I laughed at the thought of them all wondering what were going on and why they were letting the slaves go for the sake of a bundle of Damnonii cloth. That's what they got for following a whole bunch of stupid orders without having the sense to go asking questions first.

The big man who were in charge nodded at the soldiers,

and they went and fetched out four folk and marched them across the bridge. I were that glad to see them, I could've danced for joy. Ailsa were even gladder, but she managed to keep from flinging her arms around her son and shaming him in front of the other men. She just gave his arm a wee squeeze and brushed away a tear, and that were that.

'What happens now?' Bram asked when the Elders and the four free folk came walking our way and the soldiers took their bundled-up eagle back into the fort.

'The legion's got the Senate's orders to abandon the fort,' Felix said. 'Our Legate will be back at sundown, and we'll be marching south tomorrow.'

'So he don't know that we had his eagle standard while he were away?' Bram grinned. 'You think he'll ever find out?'

'Taurus and Brutus won't tell a soul, not if they want to keep their high ranks,' Felix said. 'They'll probably tell our Legate they let the slaves go free as a sign of goodwill. And as for our Standard Bearer, he's probably chewed his fingers to the bone worrying about getting the eagle back without the rest of the legion finding out, so he won't be admitting he lost the standard to anyone else.'

'They'll leave you alone then? They'll no bully you again?' Bram asked.

'My father and I are the only ones who know they lost the standard to the Damnonii. I'm pretty sure they'll be treating me like a nobleman from now on to keep me from telling anyone else!' Felix laughed.

'Come on, Felix,' his pa called. 'It's time to go.'

It were like the sun went out all of a sudden and the world turned twice as cold. 'You're going already?' I said, trying not to look like I were going to cry. 'You'll no stay for a wee bit longer?'

'I have to go and help pack up the fort supplies,' Felix said, looking even sorrier now the time had come for parting. 'I'll see you both again one day, though, I'm sure of it.'

'Ha! You'll forget us soon as the gate's closed, Roman boy,' Bram grinned, 'what with all your fancy food in there and your adventures to come.'

'That'll never happen, little man. You and Jinny will always be the best friends I've ever had.'

'Even though I near knocked your head clean off?' I joked to cover my sadness.

'If you hadn't thrown that rock, then you wouldn't have woken the stones and we'd never have found my father,' he smiled back. 'Though I'm still not entirely convinced you weren't seeing things in the dark, Jinny. You are a bit mad, after all.'

'Well at least we gave you something to remember us by and never bored you to death while you were with us, eh, Jinny?' Bram smiled, nudging me and winking. We'd no told anyone else about the stones going walking, and we never would neither. It were nice having a secret that just the three of us shared.

'Wait!' I said, just as Felix turned to go. 'Talking of things to remember us by, I clean forgot I wanted to give you this.'

I pulled a wee necklace out of my pocket and handed it to him, trying to keep from blushing and looking like a right daft wee lassie. Felix held it up to the light and looked at the charms hanging off it. They were a knot of polished wood and a round piece of stone with a hole in the middle strung on a strip of twisted leather.

'I made it from a bit of the rock I accidentally knocked out of the sacred stones, and a wee hunk of wood from the hallowed tree that the Romans left. Will you wear it and remember us, Felix?'

He grinned and hung it round his neck. 'I won't forget you both. Not ever.'

The next moment, he were gone, running up to the bridge and walking into the fort with his pa. He turned to wave as the gates shut, but I didn't see that too clear as I had something in my eyes that made them water so bad I had to blow my runny nose on the edge of my skirt.

'Alright, you two,' Pa said, coming up and clapping me and Bram on the shoulder. 'Time to go home.'

'What's the rush?' I asked, wanting to hang back for a bit and see if Felix were going to climb up onto the wall and wave from there.

'We've got a ceremony to prepare for tonight,' Pa winked. 'There's food to be cooked and cider to be tapped, so we'd best get going.'

'But Samhain's over,' Bram said, looking as puzzled as me. 'A peace treaty holding without folks going back on their word is no something you celebrate with dancing and a big feast, is it?'

'No, but a Bairntime's Passing ceremony is,' Ailsa told us. Her eyes were twinkling and she threw Pa a look like they knew something I didn't.

'Bairntime's Passing?' I blinked. 'Who's getting affirmed? Bram and his age-mates are a whole summer shy of the right time, and the lassies are all too wee to be thinking of that yet.'

'There's one lassie the Council thinks has come of age at last,' my pa grinned. It took me a moment to get what they were all hinting at. When I finally twigged, I near fell over my own two feet in surprise. 'You mean *me*?'

'Who else?' Pa smiled. 'You're no telling me you'd prefer to stay a wee lassie forever now, are you?' he teased.

I wanted so badly to smile too, but there were a lump in my throat so big it were making it hard for me to breathe. 'But our hallowed tree's all hacked to bits!' I said, trying not to cry at the thought. 'How am I meant to take my vows without the sacred oak standing witness?'

'Me and the Council have been talking on that,' Pa said, exchanging glances with Ailsa, 'and we got to thinking how the seasons change and how new things grow every year. We lost something ancient, that's true, but if we plant again this year, then sometime, many summers from now, there'll be another sacred tree standing in its place for the generations to come. Ailsa has a store of acorns from this year's hallowed tree harvest – you'll take your vows by planting a new tree in its place, Jinny.'

My mouth hung open at the thought of the honour and responsibility I were being given. 'Are you sure the Council wants to trust such a big job to the likes of me?' I gasped.

'Aye, lass,' Ailsa laughed. 'You've proved you've done a deal of growing up, and we're all right glad of that. It's no every season a couple of bairns save the tribe from war. Keep this up and you might even be an Elder one day,' she winked.

I grinned for real at that. Ailsa always said I'd turn into a mushroom afore I'd learn any sense, so that meant a lot coming from her.

'You too, Bram,' Ailsa added. 'You might even get Gregor's seat one day, if your big sister doesn't pinch it off you. In the meantime, how about you getting up on the sheiling with my Connor and learning the ropes of herding? I think that wee pony of yours is just about ready for the job of rounding up cattle and chasing sheep into line. What do you think?'

Bram looked at Pa, his eyes shining with excitement. There were nothing he'd love more than to get out of the village each day and head up to the pasturelands looking for adventure. 'Can I, Pa? Please?'

Pa struggled with the idea for a bit, then he finally gave in. 'Aye, why not, Bram. You've proved you can handle the reins of that wee pony like the best of our riders, and besides, if you stay home in the village, it won't be long afore our Jinny finds more mischief for the pair of you.'

It were strange how a heart can be full of sadness, yet fit to burst with sheer joy all at the same time. Felix might be leaving us, but he weren't the only one starting out on a big adventure.

Maybe change weren't so bad after all.

Felix

Saying goodbye was the easy part. It was leaving that was hard.

I looked back as I marched with the other officers' children behind the ranks of soldiers, taking my last look at the fort I'd called home my whole life. It had seemed so big before, but now it had shrunk to a small speck in the distance, the wall that had caused so much grief nothing more than a thin band of turf along the horizon. Soon the last of the soldiers would set fire to the wooden buildings and the palisades, making sure the Damnonii couldn't use the Romans' own defences against them if they chose to come back one day for a fresh attempt at conquest. I couldn't see that happening for a long, long time, and the thought made me smile as I marched.

There are some things stronger even than the Roman army, I thought. *Family, friendship, and the courage that comes from a sure sense of belonging. No wonder the Damnonii were willing to risk everything to defend their villages against the invaders.*

The tribespeople may have had their land taken, but they'd never been conquered, and never would be. Not as long as they loved their homeland as much as they loved life itself. My mother had tried to teach me the ways of the Damnonii, their language and their stories, but I hadn't fully understood her back then. Now I finally did. She may have chosen a Roman soldier to have a son with, and lived in the fort instead of the villages north of the wall, but deep down, she always knew where she came from and where she belonged.

I hadn't worked out yet where I belonged. But just like her, I knew exactly where I came from. I may be going to far off places, but I'd never forget the hills and fields and sacred valley of the north. No matter where I travelled, I'd always carry them with me.

I touched the strip of leather that hung round my neck, feeling the warmth of the smooth stone and the polished piece of wood beneath my fingers. Wherever I went, they'd remind me of Bram and Jinny and the adventure we'd had together. Maybe, just maybe if I remembered the legends of the Damnonii and believed in them with my whole heart like Jinny, then one day I'd hear a song on the wind and the stones would whistle me back, too.

This was my birthplace, and one day, when I was tired of marching with the army to far-off places and weary of the splendours of Rome, I'd return to this wild northern land and finally call it home.

Jinny

We stood at the top of Tintock Brae – me, Bram and Tramper – watching the Romans setting fire to their fort and the wooden stretch of fencing along the wall as they left. They were making sure to no leave a trace of their fancy defence works and watch towers behind just in case they got a notion to come marching back in the future, and so we couldn't go using their barricades and ramparts against them if they did. By the looks of them, though, they were marching away for good.

I were still wearing the crown of flowers from my Bairn-time's Passing ceremony last sundown, and my face hadn't stopped glowing yet with the pride of planting the acorn for our new hallowed tree. The other new-made women, they'd been affirmed just by dint of being old enough. But me, I'd proved my worth to the whole tribe, and no one could ever take that away from me. In many summers to come, I'd even have a grown sapling in the field for my own bairns and grandbairns to take their vows under.

'You think he'll remember us?' Bram asked, squinting into the distance where the line of marching soldiers were disappearing into the far horizon.

'Felix? Aye, he'll no forget Samhain when the walking stones led us to his pa in the dark, that's for sure. I don't think he believes what really happened that night, no yet anyhow. But one day he will,' I grinned, 'and that's the day he'll pack up his sword and the rest of his Roman armour and come marching back here to set up camp with us for good.'

'I'm still no sure myself what really happened that night,' Bram said, looking back down into the valley where the mist lay thick as a blanket over the sacred circle. 'But I know what it were that I heard. It were Ailsa what were right in the end, weren't it, Jin? She said the stones were here to help us, no harm us.'

'Aye, Bram, she were right. I whistled them back from their sleep and they came walking to show me the way to Felix's pa. If only I'd no been so scared and followed them the first night they showed up, I could've saved him from sleeping in that ditch for so long.'

'You think the stones are still awake?' Bram wondered. 'Will they come walking again?'

I looked down at the shimmering sea of mist below. Somewhere down there, just under the billowing waves of fog, a circle of stone giants stood sleeping uneasily in the dark. 'No, Bram,' I shook my head. 'I reckon they've done their job and have fallen asleep again. But don't go whistling down in the valley any time soon, though, just in case.'

'I'm no daft, Jin!' Bram laughed. 'Waking stone giants and breaking into Roman forts and pinching things is your kind of mischief, no mine.'

He were right. I were the one who had roused the stones, stolen from the Romans, and brought fire and destruction down on us all. Now the wooden fort at Caerpen Taloch that had shut us out from our own lands to the south were a riot of flames, and the whole line of the wall from east to west were burning to the ground.

It were a beautiful sight to behold.

We were free at last.

The Author

Victoria Williamson is a former teacher and full-time author from Glasgow. Her previous novels include *The Fox Girl and the White Gazelle, The Boy with the Butterfly Mind, Hag Storm,* and *War of the Wind.* She has won the Bolton Children's Fiction Award 2020/2021, The YA-aldi Glasgow Secondary School Libraries Book Award 2023, and has been shortlisted for the Week Junior Book Awards 2023, The Leeds Book Awards 2023, the James Reckitt Hull Book Awards 2021, The Trinity School Book Awards 2021, and longlisted for the ABA South Coast Book Awards 2023, the Waterstones Children's Book Prize 2020, and the Branford Boase Award 2019.

Victoria currently works part time writing KS2 books for the education company Twinkl and spends the rest of her time writing novels, and visiting schools, libraries and literary festivals to give author talks and run creative writing workshops.

Acknowledgements

This book is a product of my childhood growing up in Kirkintilloch, which was a rich tapestry of memories of countryside picnics, walks in the Gartshore Estate, by the Luggie River and up on the Campsie Hills; trips to the William Patrick Library and Auld Kirk Museum; Sunday school outings, Keynotes concerts and musicals; Kirkintilloch Players pantomimes and dramas, and a wealth of activity, music and dance clubs. It was a wonderful place to grow up, in large part because there was a strong community full of people committed to providing opportunities for children to flourish – people such as my mother, who not only volunteered as a Sunday school teacher and spent years working tirelessly as a Boys' Brigade Officer, but who dedicated her time to making my childhood as special as it could possibly be. I hope the next generation of children will weave their own magical childhood tales from the colourful threads of Kirkintilloch life, and will come to love the beauty of the changing seasons in East Dunbartonshire as much as I have.

Special thanks go to the team at Scotland Street Press, including Mirrin, Jean and Alex, who have been wonderful to work with, and who have put a huge amount of time and energy into helping make this book the best it can be. A very big thank you also to the very talented Elise Carmichael for her fantastic cover illustrations which have captured the story perfectly!

Over the last few years I've been very lucky to have

had the chance to explore the history and archaeology of my local area further through volunteering on digs with Archaeology Scotland. In order to support the wonderful work they do providing opportunities for members of the community to get involved in digs and to learn valuable conservation skills,

20% of the author royalties for this novel will be donated to Archaeology Scotland.